In the Role of

BRIE
HUTCHENS...

ALSO BY NICOLE MELLEBY

Hurricane Season

In the Role of

BRIE
HUTCHENS...

Nicole Melleby

ALGONQUIN YOUNG READERS 2020

Published by
Algonquin Young Readers
an imprint of Algonquin Books of Chapel Hill
Post Office Box 2225
Chapel Hill, North Carolina 27515-2225

a division of
Workman Publishing
225 Varick Street
New York, New York 10014

LIBRARY OF CONGRESS CATALOGING-IN-PUBLICATION DATA

Names: Melleby, Nicole, author.
Title: In the role of Brie Hutchens . . . / Nicole Melleby.
Description: First edition. | Chapel Hill, North Carolina :
Algonquin Young Readers, [2020] | Audience: Grades 4-6. |
Summary: "When strong-willed, drama-loving eighth grader
Brie Hutchens tells a lie because she isn't quite ready to come out
to her mother, she must navigate the consequences in her relationships
with her family, friends, and faith"—Provided by publisher.
Identifiers: LCCN 2019045980 | ISBN 9781616209070 (hardcover) |
ISBN 9781643750620 (ebook)
Subjects: CYAC: Coming out—Fiction. | Lesbians—Fiction. |
Honesty—Fiction. | Catholic schools—Fiction. | Schools—Fiction. |
Mothers and daughters—Fiction. | Family life—Fiction.
Classification: LCC PZ7.1.M46934 In 2020 | DDC [Fic]—dc23
LC record available at https://lccn.loc.gov/2019045980

10 9 8 7 6 5 4 3 2 1
First Edition

For Eliot,
who made me feel seen
and helped me be heard.

February

Fourteen Sundays until
the May Crowning

1.

ALL MY CHILDREN, January 1970:
A teenage Erica Kane longs to leave her small town and go to Hollywood. She's cautioned that Hollywood isn't all it's cracked up to be, but Erica isn't discouraged. She has big dreams, and she'll chase them no matter what anyone else tells her.

Brie was almost positive her mom didn't like her.

That wasn't to say her mom didn't *love* her. But Brie had a hard time believing that she *liked* her. For example, Brie didn't think she was the type of girl her mom would point at and go "Now *that* is a good girl" if they met elsewhere. Someone like Kennedy Bishop, on the other hand, was the quintessential good girl. Everyone's mom liked Kennedy Bishop.

Kennedy was destined to be the eighth grader chosen to crown Mary at Our Lady of Perpetual Help's annual celebratory mass in the spring. Brie wouldn't have cared which of her classmates was chosen—really, she wouldn't have—if it hadn't been for Kelly Monaco's boobs.

Look, first of all, Kelly Monaco was Brie's favorite soap opera star, and she *also* had really great hair. Even Brie's mom thought so. They'd had an entire conversation about it while watching *General Hospital* together. "Kelly Monaco has really great hair," her mom had said.

"She has really great everything," Brie had responded—immediately turning red. Her mom hadn't noticed.

Later Brie Googled photos of Kelly Monaco's really great hair. How was she supposed to know Kelly had done *Playboy* photos and that they would be the first thing to pop up? Really it was her mom's fault, since she had brought up Kelly Monaco's hair to begin with, and honestly Brie kept looking at the photos only because she was curious.

Well, curious . . . and maybe a little flustered.

Of course that flustered moment was when her mom decided to waltz into her room, carrying Brie's laundry and lecturing her about the need to unfold socks before throwing them in the hamper. Brie's backpack was strewn on the floor, and—miracle of miracles—her mom tripped over it, stumbling just enough to shift her eyes away from Brie's computer screen. Brie—flushed and about to burst into flame—caught sight of her religion book as it slipped out of her bag. A statue of Mary with her arms outstretched beckoned from the cover. That was the moment Brie practically shouted, "I'm going to crown Mary!"

At the time it seemed like divine intervention.

Her mom was delighted. Brie closed her browser. Crisis averted.

Well, at least *that* crisis. The bigger problem was she *hadn't* been chosen to crown Mary. No one had. The selection wouldn't happen for weeks, because, needless to say, the May Crowning was in May. The students of Our Lady of Perpetual Help still had fourteen weeks of regular masses to prepare for the eighth-grade event.

It was a big deal in Catholic school, or at least at Brie's. May was the month they honored and celebrated the Mother of God by holding a special church mass during school and inviting the rest of the parishioners to attend. The eighth-grade students got all dressed up—out of their uniforms and into their Sunday best—and the rest of the school gathered in the church to watch as the chosen one went up on the altar and put a crown made of flowers on the Mary statue's head. Since Brie had gone to OLPH since kindergarten, she'd sat through eight May Crowning masses. Now she would need to do more than sit through the ninth.

"Mrs. Dwek, I need to crown Mary," Brie said in homeroom the following Monday.

Mrs. Dwek was a small, plump woman who wore her hair piled on top of her head. Her fingers typed quickly at her laptop's keyboard, and though she never turned away from the screen, she answered Brie swiftly. "I'm glad to hear you're taking an interest, Brie. We won't be prepping for quite some time, though."

"No, you don't understand," Brie said. "I *need* to crown Mary."

This time, Mrs. Dwek did look away from her computer screen. "You know how this works. You'll all write essays, and the best essay gets to crown Mary. I'm sure Ms. Santos will have you practice in class. I know writing isn't your strongest subject."

Brie did not, unfortunately, have a strongest subject. "I think your system is flawed. The math nerds would agree."

Mrs. Dwek sighed with her entire body, as she often did while speaking to Brie. "Whoever crowns Mary reads their essay in front of the entire school, so the system is in place for a reason. And some of our strongest math students are also our strongest writers."

Brie pouted. Kennedy Bishop was good at math *and* writing.

"Go take your seat before morning prayers," Mrs. Dwek said, dismissing her.

"I can pray from right here," Brie pointed out.

Mrs. Dwek wasn't impressed. "Take your seat anyway."

Our Lady of Perpetual Help was one of a handful of Catholic schools within driving distance to Brie's house in

New Jersey. There was always a lot of talk about Catholic schools closing down, but Brie felt as though she saw as many Catholic schools in her area as Starbucks. It seemed like there was one on every corner.

But Our Lady of Perpetual Help was the smallest, and it was much too easy to stand out in a small school. Brie's dad liked to joke that Brie was a "loud fish in a little pond." For Brie, who had started OLPH as a chatty kindergartner who enjoyed being the center of attention (show-and-tell days had always been her favorite) and had worked her way up to the eighth grader she was now, making splashes was inevitable.

Unfortunately, those splashes got her a lot of phone calls home from teachers like Mrs. Dwek, which usually went like this:

Brie's mom: "Hello?"

Mrs. Dwek (because it was almost always Mrs. Dwek): "Mrs. Hutchens? It's Mrs. Dwek. I'm calling about Brie."

Brie's mom: "What did she do this time?" (Okay, she didn't really say that. But Brie could tell by the slump of her mom's shoulders and the resigned half roll of her eyes that she was thinking it.)

Mrs. Dwek: "I think we need to have a conversation about Brie's attitude, in particular her penchant for calling out in class."

Brie just had a lot to say sometimes. She might have

flown under the radar at Bayshore, the much larger *public* middle school, but she didn't blend in much at all here.

Brie didn't want to blend in, anyway. What Mrs. Dwek and her mom didn't understand was that Brie was destined for something bigger than OLPH.

Bigger than Highlands, New Jersey.

Still, she didn't want Mrs. Dwek to make one of those calls home, so she took her seat. And just as she did, the old, dusty loudspeaker—located right above the crucifix, which was right next to the American flag—crackled to life. "Good morning, students of Our Lady of Perpetual Help!" Sister Patricia, who lived across the street in the church building and was in charge of the religious studies for their school parish, always sounded so optimistic first thing in the morning. (She faded to something more like exhaustion by the end of the day.)

She continued now, her voice muffled through the speaker: "Let us begin."

That day, like every other school day, began with the Our Father.

And like every other school day, Brie mumbled along to the words on autopilot—*Our Father, who art in heaven*—tuning everything else out. Next to her, Wallace Hughes reached over to pull at a loose string from the hem of her uniform skirt, causing the pleats to bunch closer together. Her mom hadn't hemmed the skirt as high as Brie would have liked, but still, it was better than letting it hang stiff and awkwardly over her knees. "Wallace!" hissed Brie.

"Wallace, do I need to move your seat?" Mrs. Dwek asked.

"No," he responded, resting his chin on his desk. "So," he whispered as Sister Patricia moved on to the Hail Mary. *Hail Mary, full of grace . . .*

"So what?" Brie asked.

"Are you gonna come to the game or not?"

Brie sighed. Wallace sat next to her in nearly every class because alphabetically, Hughes came right before Hutchens. He was what Brie would call a "school friend," since they didn't exactly make time for each other outside of classes. Wallace was currently attempting to ruin the status quo.

If Parker Pigott hadn't thought Wallace was so cute, Brie wouldn't have bothered, but sometimes you had to make sacrifices for your best friend.

"At seven?" Brie asked. A student took over for Sister Patricia on the loudspeaker, beginning the Pledge of Allegiance, signaling that homeroom was almost over. On autopilot again, Brie and her classmates all stood at their seats, hands over their hearts. "I pledge allegiance to the flag of the United States of America."

"Seven thirty," Wallace said midpledge. He had an indent in his chin from resting it against the edge of the hard desk. He cocked his head, thick brown curls bouncing to the

9

side. "Do I need to explain hockey to you? I can do it during math. You don't pay attention anyway."

"I do so."

"Did you do the homework?"

Brie groaned as they all took their seats again. No, she had not done the homework. She'd forgotten they even had homework in math. Her mom called her forgetfulness an "organization issue."

The student on the loudspeaker began morning announcements, which never concerned Brie, since she wasn't big on the extracurriculars. Maybe she could quickly copy Wallace's homework. "Did you do it?"

"No," he said, which rendered him useless. "I got home late from practice and forgot. So, can I explain hockey to you?"

"I'll cheer when you score. I'll boo when you don't. I've got this—don't worry."

"Okay," he said, and the bell rang.

Everyone in Brie's homeroom began gathering their things. Brie grabbed her backpack, realizing it felt too light. She must have left one of her textbooks at home.

She met Parker in the hallway, like she always did.

"So?" Parker asked.

Brie rolled her eyes. "So *what*?"

"Did you tell Wallace we're coming tonight?"

"I told him *I'm* coming."

Parker's face turned bright red with only the smallest amount of needling. Parker was tall and skinny and pale. Brie sometimes thought they must look like spaghetti and a meatball when they walked down the hall together. "I know he's *your* friend. He's just . . . *so* cute, Brie!"

"*You're* my friend," Brie clarified. "And he's all yours. He's not my type."

Parker stopped to consider this, her ponytail waving back and forth as if she were still moving. "Well, then, what *is* your type?"

Parker's type was *boy*. Wallace or Jack Thomas or Javi Martinez or, or, or . . .

As for Brie . . . she was still trying to figure her type out.

(Which made her think of Kelly Monaco. Which made her think of the May Crowning, which made her think of her mom, which made her stomach hurt.)

"Just come on," Brie said with a roll of her eyes. "We're going to be late to English."

2.

ONE LIFE TO LIVE, December 1994:
Blair Cramer is tired of waiting for someone else
to make her dreams come true for her. She wants
to be rich, to be loved, but even more than that,
she wants to be respected. She's going to make it
happen one way or another.

The trouble with having a boy-crazy best friend was that sometimes, it made Brie's lunch period exhausting.

It should go without saying that lunch was Brie's favorite period, especially on days when she had to suffer through English, math, *and* religion first. Her stomach was growling, even though her mom made her and her brother the same turkey sandwiches every single day—always with two clementines on the side no matter how many times Brie asked for potato chips. The faculty used to make them say grace together in the cafeteria, but that had stopped around third grade. It wasn't worth the amount of time it took to get them all to *quiet down already!* and Brie appreciated being able to dive right in, unlike at home during dinner.

She was crust-deep into her sandwich when Jack Thomas—the reason Parker beelined to this particular lunch table—held out a pack of gum to the boys he was sitting with. Gum was *strictly forbidden*. Their teachers made such a big deal of it that in the second grade, Brie had combed through the internet for some proof that Jesus or John the Baptist or even God himself had declared chewing gum was some sort of sin.

Since Parker loved a bad boy—especially one with Jack Thomas's "cute little beauty mark" on the tip of his chin—the exchange of gum immediately caught her eye.

Jack noticed. "You want one?" he asked.

Parker nodded. Brie snorted a laugh before she could stop herself. Parker and Jack both shot her looks—Jack confused and Parker flustered—and Brie waved them off. "Sorry. Just . . . thinking about Mrs. Dwek's . . . dog."

Jack made a face. "Mrs. Dwek has a dog?"

"Yup. Sure. A puggle."

Without giving Jack any more time to question it, Parker quickly reached for the stick of gum. "Thank you!" she said, cheeks and neck pink.

Jack just shrugged and turned back to the boys. Brie shook her head as Parker clutched the stick of gum. She knew Parker would never chew that particular piece. For one, Parker turned beet red and nearly cried if a teacher yelled at someone *near* her, and Brie couldn't imagine what she would do if a teacher yelled *at* her. For two, Parker was sentimental like that.

She would keep Jack Thomas's stick of gum for the rest of the school year, at the very least.

Which was soap-worthy dramatic.

But it was also, if Brie was honest, kind of nice.

She'd never had strong enough feelings for a boy to make her want to hoard a piece of gum. Not even close. And sometimes—well, most times—it made Brie mad that Parker could feel that way for so many boys when Brie would settle for just . . . one.

One best-friend-and-mom-appeasing crush.

"Those earrings look a little big, Brie." Mrs. Dwek always just *appeared* in front of a table when she was on lunch duty. It was like she Apparated from one end of the cafeteria to the other.

Brie tugged at her admittedly large hoop earring. The thing about Catholic-school uniforms was that they were all the same. The girls wore the same button-up blouses, the same color of tights, the same black shoes, and the same skirts (though they varied in length, depending on how generous their parents were with hemming). And every piece of clothing was shapeless and stiff. But Parker always wore brightly colored hair clips that looked nice with the light blue of her

14

glasses, Deena Yousef always tried to get away with wearing mascara, and Shaun Frankel wore his amber-bead necklace.

Everyone had *something*. Brie's something was Erica Kane–approved big earrings. A real soap-star look.

"I've worn them before" was Brie's best defense. Why couldn't Mrs. Dwek zero in on Jack's gum chewing instead?

"Doesn't mean they aren't too big," Mrs. Dwek replied, in that way she always did to undercut Brie's best excuses.

Brie was about to defend her style choices, but then someone caught her eye.

Oh no. What is he *doing in here?*

At the front of the cafeteria, for everyone to see, two maintenance men were fixing the loudspeaker, which was, of course, above the cafeteria's own crucifix. One of the maintenance men was removing the crucifix so it would be out of the way while they worked on the speaker. The other was scanning the cafeteria.

Brie knew exactly what he was looking for: *her*.

Because that maintenance man was her dad.

"You know what, Mrs. Dwek? You are absolutely correct. I'll go to the bathroom and take them off immediately," Brie said. "Come help me, Parker."

Parker stared at her for a moment, eyes squinting behind her glasses. "Why do you need to go to the bathroom to—"

She stopped talking the moment Brie ducked under the cafeteria table to reemerge on the other side beside her.

Brie grabbed Parker's hand—still clutching Jack Thomas's stick of gum—and offered Mrs. Dwek, who was as confused as Parker, a smile. "Be right back!" Brie said and quickly dragged Parker away.

Parker wasn't the best cover. She was the tallest kid in school, and Brie's dad had known Parker since they were seven. But at least if he saw them and said hello, well, Parker already knew he was working there.

The rest of her classmates did not, and Brie wanted to keep it that way.

They'd almost made it out of the cafeteria—because of course she would *almost* make it—when she heard her dad call out, "Brie!" He smiled, crow's-feet crinkling in the corners of his eyes and his cheeks puffing out.

It was his first year working at her school. Brie's mom had somehow struck a deal where her dad would work at the school and Brie's tuition would be less expensive. They'd been having a difficult time paying recently since her dad had lost his real job.

His real job that had kept him out of OLPH and away from the cafeteria, where he was holding a crucifix and waving to Brie.

"Can't talk! Bathroom emergency!" she called behind her as she raced through the cafeteria doors, pulling Parker behind her.

Brie *really* hoped that at the end of the day, when she met her dad in the maintenance office after school, he wouldn't mention the fact that she had obviously dodged him. It wasn't like she could tell him why she didn't want to chat in front of all her classmates.

Brie always had to wait an extra twenty minutes after dismissal before her dad got there. But she didn't mind so long as they made it home in time for Brie to watch *General Hospital* with her mom. Besides, the maintenance staff always had a box of Munchkins from Dunkin' on the table.

She popped a powdered Munchkin into her mouth just as her dad appeared at the door. "Hey, kid. You ready to go?"

With her cheeks full of doughnut, she mumbled, "Yep!"

"You know I can always just get you from your classroom instead, right?" he asked, as he did almost every day. "You don't need to wait in this dank office."

Brie swallowed her Munchkin. It went down hard. "It's okay. I don't mind."

The ride home was quiet, which had been the case lately when they left school. Once home, Brie dropped her backpack on the floor, untucked her shirt from her plaid skirt, kicked off her shoes, and rolled off her tights as she made her way into the living room. Ever since she'd started getting rides home with her dad instead of taking the bus, she'd been cutting it close to missing her favorite show. *General Hospital* was already on the TV, and Brie stepped into the room just in time to hear the *smack!* as Sonny Corinthos's current wife, Carly, slapped him. Brie loved this show. "Oh my *God*, what did he do this time?"

"Carly found out about Mexico," Brie's mom said, not taking her eyes off the TV. It was her favorite show, too. She was already wearing her name tag for work. Some days she got home from her part-time shift at the mall right before *General Hospital* started; other times she had to leave for work right after. Luckily, she was almost always able to watch, which made Brie happy. It was pretty much the only thing they did together. Except when her mom dragged her to go shopping, but those outings usually ended in arguments. "She's being a little dramatic about it, if you ask me," her mom continued.

Brie loved soap operas *because* they were so dramatic. They were full of characters with giant personalities who made terrible mistakes and terrible decisions and still managed to fall in love and be awesome. Brie, if she was being honest, admired all of them. She wanted to *be* them. So much so that the thing she was most looking forward to now that she was in the eighth grade was the spring play. Well, that and being one step closer to graduating middle school, one step closer to an opportunity that could help her achieve her dream.

"I would have slapped him, too," Brie said, taking a seat next to her mom on the sofa.

Brie's mom laughed. "Yeah, well, you do have Carly's temper. I went shopping, if you want a snack."

"Pop-Tarts?" Brie asked.

"In the cabinet," her mom answered as the camera pulled in on Carly's tearstained face. "Have *one*, Brie."

"They put two Pop-Tarts in one package so you eat them both," Brie pointed out.

"You don't need to eat both," her mom said.

Brie did not share her mom and older brother's body type. They also did not share eye or hair color (though Brie knew her mom dyed hers—she'd seen enough old photographs to tell).

But when Brie and her mom sat in the living room, watching their soaps, Brie forgot they had so little in common. Not many of her friends' moms had time to sit and watch TV with their daughters, and although her mom would be watching whether or not Brie was in the room—and vice versa for Brie—it still was something. It was *their* thing. The thing they had done for as long as Brie could remember.

She remembered being too small to really understand what was going on. Too small to see over the coffee table from where she sat on the carpet in the living room, playing with her toys, peeking up over the edge to watch these characters her mom seemed so fond of, trying to figure out what, exactly, made her so fond of them. She remembered listening to the dialogue and repeating it back to herself in her bedroom mirror, remembered how much it made her mom laugh the first time she did it when her mom was around.

She remembered asking questions and her mom saying she was too young to understand. That was frustrating, so Brie paid closer attention and kept asking questions, until suddenly her mom stopped saying she was too young and started answering her. Until Brie didn't have to ask anymore, and they had conversations about what was happening instead. All the while Brie never stopped repeating the dialogue into her mirror at night.

Brie's cell phone buzzed, and she picked it up to read the incoming text from Parker. "Parker's mom is picking me up at seven," Brie said. "We're going to the boys' hockey game at the Armory."

"Oh really?" her mom said, perfectly shaped eyebrows disappearing into blond bangs. "For a particular boy, or . . . ?"

It was a leading question, one Brie, at thirteen, was already used to. She felt her cheeks turn warm, and she shifted uncomfortably in her seat. "Stop, no. Just to watch the game."

"Didn't know you were such a hockey fan."

"I'm a fan of hanging out with Parker and drinking hot cocoa," Brie countered. "Not everything is about boys."

"There's nothing wrong with liking boys, Brie," her mom

said as Brie continued blushing. "High school is around the corner, and there are homecoming dances and proms and—"

"I'm still in eighth grade!" shouted Brie. "None of that even matters yet. *Stop*."

Her mom looked at her as if she'd sprouted an extra head, her wide, defined mouth curved down at the corners. Her fingers reached for the pendant that hung around her neck, sliding it back and forth along its chain. "Why are you yelling? We're just having a conversation."

"I don't want to talk about this."

"This is why it's so difficult to talk to you—you can't just have a conversation."

"Mom, just forget it!"

Neither one of them said anything after that as *General Hospital* played out on the TV in front of them. Brie could hardly pay attention. Kelly Monaco came on the screen, with her dark pretty hair and a mischievous smile, and Brie sank into her seat, distractedly picking at her fingernails. Her mom's hand was still toying with the Mother of God pendant she never took off.

Brie looked away from the TV. Focused on her chipped nail polish instead. (The nail polish Mrs. Dwek had yet to notice.) Brie still had to tell her mom she lied about crowning Mary, and the part that made her stomach hurt was trying to figure out what she could possibly say when her mom inevitably asked her why she lied in the first place.

I didn't want you to see me looking at another woman's boobs, and I don't want you to know why I get upset every time you ask me about boys.

"You know you can talk to me about anything," her mom suddenly said.

Brie wondered if she really meant it.

Luckily, her dad chose that moment to walk back in through the front door, a small stack of mail in his hands. "Trevor!" he shouted up the stairs toward Brie's older brother's bedroom, which Trevor pretty much never left. "I can see your tire prints on the grass again! You need to turn more carefully!"

Brie's dad came into the living room and handed Brie's mom most of the stack, pressing a kiss on her forehead as he passed by. He held out a thin-looking pamphlet to Brie. "Looks like something came in the mail for you."

"Me?" Brie said, taking it from him. She never got any mail.

When she saw what it was, she let out a shrill screech, jumping off the couch and causing her mom to exasperatedly shout, "Gabrielle! Talk about being dramatic."

Brie dramatically rolled her eyes. Dramatics were exactly what she needed! She'd almost forgotten she'd sent away for the brochure, but here it was, right in her hands, in gold and purple lettering: *Monmouth County Performing Arts.*

This was why she couldn't wait for graduation. It was Brie's lifelong dream to go to MCPA. Well, ever since she'd learned about the performing arts high school when its students came to her fourth-grade class in full costume to promote their latest show. Brie had gone home and immediately begged her mom to take her to it. The two of them had gone to MCPA's big spring show every year since.

MCPA was a high school dedicated solely to the arts—a school where she could learn how to be as good an actress as her favorite soap stars on TV—and the brochure had lists of classes that included theater and television and film acting. It talked about the special guests that had visited in the past, including Broadway actress Kelli O'Hara, Monmouth County's own resident composer Tim Arnold, and—"*Oh my gosh!*"—soap opera actress Melissa Reeves. There was even a list on the back of the brochure with the names of students who had gone on to successful acting careers postgraduation.

"I *have* to go here!" Brie said, which was exactly what she'd told Parker in the fourth grade the second the high school students had finished their short promotional performance.

"Let me see that," her mom said, and as she reached for the brochure, Brie didn't let go. "Why did we get this?"

"I filled out a form online," Brie said, flipping through the brochure for information about auditions. "I need to do the application next, but I'll need a credit card. I think the fee's like fifty dollars."

Her mom exchanged a glance with her dad. "Brie, wait. Don't you think this is something you should talk to us about first?"

Brie didn't like the tone of her mom's voice. "We talk about it every year. We go to their show every year."

Another parental exchange of glances.

"What?" Brie asked.

Brie's mom kept her eyes on her dad, but he didn't say anything. She sighed and said, "We can't afford this."

"It's only fifty dollars."

"The *school*. We can't afford this school."

"We can't afford OLPH, either," Brie pointed out. "Dad can work out a deal with them, too, maybe."

"Brie."

"I can at least audition, can't I? And we can go from there."

"Brie."

"It's my *dream*, Mom!"

"*Brie!*"

"*What?*"

The room fell silent, except for the conversation on the TV in the background. An ex trying to reconcile with the man who always had her heart. A conversation steadily turning into a bitter argument between an ex-boyfriend and ex-girlfriend. Brie's dad reached for the remote and turned the TV off.

"The answer is no," her mom said. "It's a lot of money for a program that narrows your focus too much. The odds of getting this kind of work, to shell out this kind of money for you to end up with an uncertain future—"

"It's not uncertain," Brie said, then looked at her dad. "You guys always say to follow our dreams. Is that all crap?"

"Brie, just hear your mother out."

"No. She never hears *me* out."

"Hey, watch your tone," her mom said. "And how can you expect us to be okay with spending money we don't have on this school? How can you ask your father to make more sacrifices for you to attend another expensive school, when you barely put in an effort at the one you're already at? Your report card last quarter was atrocious."

"I didn't fail anything!"

"Mediocre grades for mediocre effort," her mom said.

Brie looked to her dad for support, but he just cringed in a way that meant *you know she's right*, because she was. Brie had a backpack full of unfinished homework and a grammar test she'd gotten a C-minus on since she hadn't studied for it.

The words slipped from her mouth as desperately and as easily as they had the day before: "But I'm going to crown Mary!"

Her mom's face softened, her hand reaching to rub her pendant again.

Brie swallowed and kept going. "And I'm auditioning for the eighth-grade spring play. If I get in and show you I can be good at this . . . and if I put more of an effort into school and everything . . . and since I'm . . ." She swallowed again. "Since I'm crowning Mary. Can't you think about it? Just a little?" She turned again to appeal to her dad. "Please?"

One more exchange of glances, followed by her dad saying, "I guess we can think about it, Erin, can't we?"

Her mom sighed and frowned but said, "Okay. We'll think about it."

Brie considered that a win.

Even if she still had to find a way to crown Mary.

3.

AS THE WORLD TURNS, November 1985:
Lily Walsh meets her mother's new stable hand,
a boy not much older than Lily. Holden more than
gets on Lily's nerves at first, but she can't seem
to stay away. It takes a while, but eventually, they
manage to become friends.

"I *have* to stay on my mom's good side until I can audition
for MCPA," Brie said to Parker as they climbed the bleachers of the Red Bank Armory Ice Complex, looking for good
seats.

"When are spring-play tryouts?" Parker asked as she sat
down. "Do you think you can get a good part?"

Brie sat next to her, shifting her weight on the cool metal
seat. "*Auditions*. And I hope so, but right now I'm more worried about the whole May Crowning thing."

Parker shrugged. "Maybe you'll get lucky. Or maybe you should just fess up now. You can work on all the other school things. Crowning Mary wouldn't be the deciding factor, would it?"

"It's keeping my mom's focus away from all the flaws. It's like it's the one thing that keeps her thinking that I'm, you know, not a heathen," Brie said.

Parker snort-laughed and took off her glasses to wipe the fog away. It was cold in the ice rink. Brie wished she'd thought to wear gloves. The game hadn't yet started, and the teams were skating around the ice, taking practice shots on their own goalies. Brie spotted Wallace and waved, but she wasn't sure if he could see her through his helmet.

"Wallace is so cute." Parker sighed.

Brie wasn't the only one who could be dramatic. For someone who barely spoke to boys, Parker could be prone to theatrics where they were concerned. She pointed at Jack, who was currently lining up his shot. "Jack is so cute, too. I can't believe he offered me gum today. *Me!* Of all people!"

"Please tell me you don't have some sort of Jack Thomas gum shrine in your bedroom now."

They were beginning to tread dangerous conversational territory, as far as Brie was concerned. These particular talks always ended with Parker prodding Brie to say who *she* thought was cutest. Brie always just said the first boy that popped into her head.

Last year she'd accidentally blurted out the name of their seventh-grade science teacher, Mr. Devane. It'd taken her half the school year to live that down, especially since she'd been so embarrassed about it that she'd turned bright red anytime he called on her to answer a question.

She really, really did not like when Parker dragged her into those conversations.

Brie, wanting to make sure they moved on from that particular topic, rubbed her hands together and blew hot breath onto them—a little more dramatically than necessary—and stood. "It's freezing. I'm getting us cocoa," she announced. Parker, her eyes still glued on the skating boys, just handed Brie a few dollar bills.

Brie walked past parents, other kids from school, and a bunch of kids she didn't know as she made her way down the bleachers. The boys' hockey team was made up of students from a bunch of schools in the area, and they won a lot. Since not many of OLPH's sports teams won anything, plenty of people went to these games. This meant, of course, that the line for the concession stand was long, so Brie took her place, hid her hands in the warmth of her armpits, and waited.

And waited. And waited.

Brie did not have the patience of a saint.

"Oh, wow, the line is long," someone behind Brie said.

"Yeah, too long," Brie said, turning around and coming face-to-face with Kennedy Bishop. "Oh. It's you."

Kennedy had on a long gray sweater and jeans. Her dark hair spilled out from under a purple knit cap, framing cheeks that were pink from the cool air. Seeing Kennedy in jeans, instead of her pleated uniform skirt, felt kind of like seeing a stripeless zebra. She and Kennedy didn't run into each other much outside of class.

"Hi, Brie," Kennedy said.

Brie would bet that Kennedy *did* have the patience of a saint. She had all the other qualities, after all.

She's pretty, too, Brie thought as they stood closer together than they ever had. *Her hair is dark and thick like Kelly Monaco's.* The line moved forward, and Brie was relieved to step out of Kennedy's space.

"Who are you here with?" Kennedy asked.

"Parker," Brie answered. "Wallace invited us."

"Oh, cool. I'm here with my family. My brother's one of the seventh graders on the team. We come to all the games."

Brie's brother was as mediocre at everything as Brie was. She wondered if Kennedy's younger brother was as good at everything as Kennedy was. When she opened her mouth to ask, Kennedy took another step forward, nearly colliding with Brie. "Oh! Sorry," Kennedy said as Brie reached out to grasp her shoulders and steady her. "The line moved—I assumed you'd move with it."

Kennedy's breath was warm on Brie's face, which should have grossed her out, but it smelled pretty nice and Brie was pretty cold. Kennedy's coat was warm where Brie was holding her arm, and she almost didn't want to let go. "I'm getting Parker and me hot cocoas," Brie found herself saying. "Do you want one?"

Kennedy gave her a mischievous smile that reminded Brie of her favorite soap character. "You buying?" she asked.

Brie's laughter felt more like the exhaling of a balloon. "I actually don't think I have enough money."

"*Next*," the woman behind the concession-stand counter said. Brie suddenly realized she was next in line. "What do you need?"

"Three hot chocolates," Kennedy said from beside her. Brie was about to object, but Kennedy pulled off one of her gloves to fish her hand deep into her pocket and took out a crumpled stack of dollar bills. "My treat."

"Oh," Brie said, her cheeks growing warm even though she was still cold. "No, it's cool—you don't have to."

Kennedy handed the lady the money anyway.

They got their hot cocoas, and the steam from the two cups in Brie's hands wafted up to her face, already making her feel much warmer. She smiled at Kennedy, who held her own cup close. Neither one of them moved to walk away, and Brie wasn't sure what she was supposed to do next. "Well, thanks," she said. "I guess I'll see you at school Monday."

Kennedy's smile faded a bit. "Oh, right. Yeah, okay. See you Monday."

They hovered a minute longer, and Brie shifted her weight on her toes, wondering why Kennedy was still standing there. Brie finally decided to make the first move and turned to head back to the bleachers. She felt bad about leaving. She wasn't sure why.

Brie found her seat, which seemed a lot smaller. The bleachers were much more crowded now that the game was about to start. Brie handed Parker her hot cocoa and money. "Kennedy Bishop bought our drinks," she said.

"She did?" Parker asked, the steam from her cocoa immediately fogging her glasses. "Huh."

Huh *is right.*

Parker let out an excited squeal as the referee dropped the puck and the game began. Brie didn't know how Parker could tell which player was Wallace or which one was Jack—they all just skated around in clumps of colored jerseys—but she figured Parker didn't really care. Brie herself didn't care much about hockey—her mom had been right about that—so instead of watching the ice, she looked around the bleachers.

Brie didn't realize she was looking for Kennedy until she spotted her purple cap. Kennedy was sitting with her parents and younger sister, sipping her hot cocoa, as they cheered on her brother. (Which blurry colored jersey was Kennedy's brother, she had no idea.)

Brie felt . . . weird about their concession-stand encounter. She found herself forgetting about the boys on the ice and thinking instead about the warmth of Kennedy's breath and how not gross it was to feel it on her face and how Brie liked Kennedy's pink cheeks and dark hair. Did Kennedy want to sit with her and Parker? Did Brie wish she had invited her? Brie looked away and focused instead on the warmth of the hot cocoa in her hands, the hot cocoa that Kennedy had bought her.

It was weird to think about this, wasn't it? Brie hated Kennedy. (Or, at least, she was jealous of Kennedy—which was basically the same thing—because Kennedy was everything Brie's mom wanted *her* to be.)

Anyway, at the very least, she didn't *like* Kennedy.

Everyone around her suddenly erupted into a commotion of cheers that startled Brie into nearly dropping her cup. Their team had scored, and Parker was standing, jumping up and down as everyone around them whistled and whooped in excitement.

Even through the waving arms—and Parker's jumping body—Brie could see Kennedy in the crowd, smiling at the excitement on the ice, her hands still wrapped tight around her cocoa and a strand of hair falling into her face. Her little sister was tugging on her mom's arm, trying to get her attention, and her dad was shouting encouragement at the team.

As she sat there surrounded by her family, Kennedy looked kind of alone. Brie should have invited her to sit with them.

But she didn't. Because Kennedy always raised her hand. Because Kennedy always did her homework, always got first place in everything, and probably always—without having to try—made her mom super proud.

Brie did not like Kennedy.

Did she?

4.

GENERAL HOSPITAL, January 2009:
After screwing up everything in her life, Sam McCall decides to figure out who she is. She wants to apply for a PI license, even though her then boyfriend, Lucky Spencer, is dead set against it. She does it anyway.

In church on Sunday, when Brie would usually daydream about a whole lot of nothing, she instead spent that time trying to bargain with God.

She said her *amen*s in the right places. She sang the songs aloud. She even knelt without complaining. She did everything her mom expected her to, all the while having a silent conversation with God. Brie tried to convince him she would do something really saintlike if only he would let her be picked to crown Mary.

Her mom, of course, knelt and stood and knelt again as if angels themselves were aiding her movements. She never needed a cue to say an *amen* in the right place, and she knew all her prayers flawlessly. And after Communion, when Trevor always looked like he was half-asleep, and Brie always knelt against the pew with her thoughts drifting, their mom was always so . . . *into* it all.

Brie couldn't help but watch as her mother bowed her head into her clasped hands, eyes shut, having a silent moment with, well, God, Brie supposed. A moment that seemed so . . . intimate, and real, and important, if the creases in her mom's forehead were any indication. Her mom's hand reached for the pendant around her neck and held it so tightly, Brie had to look away. It made her blush, because it seemed like such a private moment, and Brie, for the life of her, just didn't know how to replicate it.

Especially since her mind kept wandering, and every time it did, it mostly made her think about the reason she was in this mess to begin with, which was Kelly Monaco's pretty hair and pretty face and pretty . . . well, *everything*.

She doubted her mom *or* God would appreciate that.

At school on Monday, Brie was resigned to the fact that prayer would not save her and that she would have to achieve her goal the hard way: paying extra-close attention in English class and hoping that Ms. Santos would teach her exactly how to write a winning May Crowning essay.

Her mom always told her she could achieve anything if only she applied herself. It was time to put that theory to the test.

So there Brie sat, next to Wallace as always, listening the best she could as Ms. Santos began her lesson. She had her notebook opened to a blank page and everything. No doodles, even.

"Okay," Ms. Santos began. "What makes a great speech?"

That sounded like a good note-taking header. Brie went to write it down, but of course her pen barely got through the *What* before it ran out of ink. She groaned. "I'm already doomed."

Wallace gave her the side-eye.

"Lend me a pen," Brie whispered.

He held up his pencil, the metal end of which was chewed flat. "I've only got this."

Brie sighed. So much for taking notes.

She glanced around the classroom. At least all the other students in her class looked equally as clueless or bored. Wallace put his chin down on his desk, his eyes half-droopy. Parker was across the room, carving little figurines out of pencil erasers. Shaun Frankel was tugging on his ripped shoe, making it worse. His *Minecraft* socks, which Mrs. Dwek would surely have a thing or two to say about, poked out from his pant leg. Javi Martinez had his eyes closed against his clasped hands, elbows resting on his desk, but Brie highly doubted he was deep in prayer. Unless maybe he was asking God to make this class go by more quickly.

Even Kennedy Bishop, who sat in the front row, didn't have her hand raised to loudly volunteer an answer to Ms. Santos's question. That made Brie feel a little better.

Kennedy turned around and caught Brie's gaze. Brie smiled, and Kennedy smiled back, and Brie immediately looked back down at her English textbook, her fingers playing with the corner of the page.

"How about this," Ms. Santos continued. "Who here can name a famous speech?"

"You can't handle the truth!" shouted Shaun Frankel from the center of the room. Like Brie, Shaun called out a lot in class, but unlike Brie (at least in her opinion), he was always annoying.

A few students laughed as Ms. Santos smirked at him in the way that always made Brie's cheeks hot. Ms. Santos was Brie's youngest teacher, and unlike most of the others, Ms. Santos still had patience for laughter. She wore cute dresses that always had pockets, and her head was covered with short wild curls. "Shouting out aside, Shaun's not wrong. 'You can't handle the truth' is, actually, a famous movie speech. But who can, after raising their hand, name a non-movie speech?"

A few students raised their hands, Kennedy included. Ms. Santos called on Deena Yousef. "Martin Luther King Jr.'s speech?" she said.

"Yes, great," Ms. Santos responded. "The 'I Have a Dream' speech."

"Notice how half the class turned to look at me," Wallace mumbled. He was one of three black kids in their grade, and the only one in Brie's English class.

Brie turned to look at him as he sighed. She gave him a look of sympathy that felt more like a cringe. She obviously wasn't the only one who thought their small school was stifling.

Ms. Santos continued on, and Brie tried again to focus, even if she didn't see how any of this was supposed to help her. She raised her hand.

Ms. Santos looked surprised. "Yes, Brie?"

"I thought we were supposed to be writing essays, not speeches."

Ms. Santos tapped her nose. "Patience. But you raise a good point. Now that we've passed our grammar unit, I know you're all ready to dive into essay structure. We *are* going to spend the rest of the school year focusing on that, especially in preparation for the May Crowning in a few months."

Shaun grumbled in his seat.

"Okay, maybe not all of you are exactly eager to dive in," Ms. Santos amended. "That being said, why start with speeches?"

Ms. Santos was the type of teacher who never answered questions without trying to get the class to answer them first. Sometimes Brie wished she would cut to the chase.

Kennedy raised her hand. Brie sank in her seat, feeling her cheeks grow warm.

"Go ahead, Kennedy," Ms. Santos said.

"Someone's going to have to read their essay out loud, right?" Kennedy said. "So it's sort of like a speech, isn't it?"

"Exactly," Ms. Santos said.

Brie knew the saying *there are no stupid questions*, but she found herself feeling pretty stupid anyway.

"And we're going to spend the next couple of months reading essays and listening to speeches and talking about the techniques used in both. By the end of this term, you'll all be pros."

Brie groaned again.

"What?" Wallace whispered.

"I *have* to crown Mary," Brie said. "Paying attention was supposed to help, but this all sounds exhausting already."

Wallace laughed. "Yeah right. Someone like Kennedy Bishop or Anthony Esposito is going to end up crowning Mary. No offense."

Some taken, Brie thought. Even if she knew he was right. There wasn't an award or an academic privilege won at OLPH that didn't go to Kennedy or Anthony.

Mostly to Kennedy.

"Here's what I want you all to do for homework," Ms. Santos said, resulting in a chorus of sighs and groans. "Go home and listen to speeches. All different kinds. Historical speeches, movie speeches, sports-related speeches. Any kind you want—just make sure you listen to a bunch. Then I want you to make a list of at least five things that you think a great speech needs to have. And don't Google for an answer! I want you to come up with these lists on your own. Sound good?"

Ms. Santos received more sighs and groans in return.

When lunch rolled around, Brie talked Parker into accompanying her to find Ms. Brophy, even though Parker would have much rather gone straight to Jack Thomas's table in the cafeteria. Parker grumbled the whole way—that is, until they walked into Javi Martinez.

Literally walked into. Parker had turned a corner and collided with him. "Whoa," Javi said as he did a little spin move to avoid falling, brown paper lunch bag crinkling in his hand. He wore his shirtsleeves rolled all the way up, skinny arms on full display, a style Sister Patricia in particular was not fond of. "You good?"

Parker, beet red, responded to him in a voice that was about an octave higher than her usual one. "I'm good!"

With a satisfied nod, Javi headed to the cafeteria.

Brie gave Parker a once-over to make sure she wasn't having a stroke. "You good?" mocked Brie.

Parker sighed. "He's so nice, isn't he?"

"Yeah, yeah," Brie said. "Let's get moving."

Ms. Brophy was the eighth-grade art teacher, the seventh-grade religion teacher, *and* in charge of the drama club. Sure, their school was small, but Brie could only assume the Catholic diocese was cheap. Ms. Brophy's office was basically a supply closet, though she didn't seem to mind. Brie knocked on the open door, even though Ms. Brophy could see anyone who approached it from where she sat at her cramped desk covered in art stuff. "Hello, girls," Ms. Brophy greeted them. "Come on in."

Brie and Parker stayed in the doorway.

"We were just wondering—"

"We?" Parker interrupted.

"Yes, both of us," Brie said. "Anyway, spring-play sign-ups are supposed to be today, but we didn't see a sign-up sheet anywhere."

Ms. Brophy nearly leaped out of her seat. "Of course! I almost forgot! Great that you want to be involved—you're certainly one of our spunkier students, Brie."

Brie was certain that was meant to be a compliment.

"And Parker, well, theater will help you spread those wings, speak up a bit more." Ms. Brophy ignored Parker's protests as she opened her desk drawers filled with paper and art supplies. Brie was glad they'd waited in the door-way. There was even less space in the tiny office with all the commotion. "Here it is," Ms. Brophy said and handed them a blank sheet of printer paper with SPRING PLAY typed neatly at the top.

Brie reached for a marker that was on top of Ms. Brophy's desk.

"What's the play?" Parker asked.

"Oh, you're in for a treat! We're doing Snow White. Lots of parts available, seven entire dwarfs!" Ms. Brophy responded. "But you'll hear all about it Friday when you both come to auditions."

"Auditions?" Parker practically screeched.

"You'll both need to prepare a monologue. I have some here somewhere if you need help choosing." Ms. Brophy began opening and closing drawers again.

Brie held out her hands to stop her. "That's okay. We'll figure it out."

She held the sign-up sheet against the wall and wrote down her name.

5.

DAYS OF OUR LIVES, January 1991:
Carrie Brady is leaving town to be with her mom.
She's sad about leaving, and so is her dad. But
he tells her that he would never ever stand in the
way of anything that's important to her.

Brie's dad was quiet when he met her in the maintenance office later. He was still quiet as they got in the car and drove home. "Is something wrong?" Brie asked when he didn't switch the radio station like he usually did once a commercial started.

He patted her knee. "Just tired," he said.

But when he didn't comment on his favorite WHAT'S YOUR BEEF? billboard, didn't complain about the loud muffler in the car next to them when they were stopped at a red light, and kept wiping his face with his hands, Brie started to squirm in her seat. "Why're you so tired?" she asked quietly after the second commercial break on the radio.

Her dad sighed, stretched his fingers out over the steering wheel. He said nothing. Brie thought maybe he hadn't heard her, maybe she should repeat herself.

But then he reached over to pat her leg again. "It's just been a lot ever since they let me go."

The company Brie's dad had worked at for as long as Brie could remember had "downsized," according to Brie's mom. Which meant that only a select few got to keep their jobs. Brie's dad was not one of them. "You have your new job now, though. At the school."

His smile was tight. "That I do."

They pulled into the driveway behind Trevor's car. Brie wasn't allowed to drive with her brother. Her mom said it was because he was too inexperienced, and Brie figured if he was going to get into an accident, her mom wanted to keep the odds in their favor that they'd still have at least one kid. Honestly, Brie didn't blame her; she kind of agreed. The grass along the edges of the driveway was flattened and muddy from where Trevor kept driving onto it.

Brie expected her dad to comment on the grass like he always did, especially since Trevor was sitting right there in the living room with their mom when they walked inside. But her dad didn't say anything. He went right upstairs.

Her mom noticed and followed him without a word of greeting to Brie. Brie watched her ascend the stairs behind him, and she hovered at the door, not really sure if she should go turn on *General Hospital* like usual or wait to see if her mom came back down.

"He's depressed," Trevor said, cutting through Brie's indecision.

"No he's not," she responded. "He was fine yesterday."

"He's depressed and Mom's stressed," Trevor said. His long, gangly body was draped over the couch, and Brie wanted to push him off, wanted him to go back to hibernating in his bedroom, far away from the sanctuary of where she watched her soaps.

"I heard him talking to Mom," Trevor continued, oblivious to Brie's mood. "He knows he embarrasses you."

"That's not true."

"Yes it is."

"Yeah, well, maybe you should stop ruining his grass with your stupid driving," Brie snapped back. "He's not a huge fan of that, either, if you haven't noticed."

"Whatever, Brie."

"He's just tired!"

Brie didn't want to argue with her brother. She didn't want to wait for her mom, either, so she ran upstairs. She could watch *General Hospital* on the streaming app later. She had homework to do. She had to write a list for

English and find a monologue for auditions. Which were both important.

But as she sat at her computer, Brie got more and more frustrated. She should have been watching *General Hospital* with her mom, and her dad should have been telling Trevor to stop driving on his lawn, and she didn't want to think about that. Because *nothing* was wrong, and Trevor was just annoying. Her dad was tired. He worked all day, and the students were loud and maintenance work was hard.

Brie almost went back downstairs to tell Trevor everything she was thinking and to take the TV back from him so she could watch her soap.

But then she had an idea.

Soap opera scenes were emotional and powerful and dramatic. They were *perfect*. Brie pulled up Google and typed *soap opera monologues* in the search bar. A ton of scenes popped up. Brie pumped a fist in the air. This she could do. This would help her finish her homework *and* help her wow Ms. Brophy at her audition, which would help her wow her mom with her performance in the play, which might even impress the May Crowning committee. And then, with the approval of everyone in her life, she could move on to wow the judges at the performing arts school auditions.

Most of the scenes that came up in her search were from before Brie started watching soaps, because they were from before Brie was born. A lot of them were from soaps that had been canceled years ago. But Brie was still familiar with a lot of the characters and even sort of familiar with the story lines. Soap operas had long, complicated histories. Brie loved trying to connect all the dots, loved the complicated tangle of relationships.

She watched Robin Scorpio's emotional speech during *General Hospital*'s Nurses Ball. She watched in awe as Karen Wolek broke down on the witness stand on *One Life to Live*. She watched Reva Shayne's "Slut of Springfield" speech on *Guiding Light*. She couldn't look away, getting caught in a YouTube spiral, watching old scenes that had no monologues in them at all just because she wanted to see more. She started a new Google Doc to keep track of the ones that stood out, copying and pasting links and jotting down notes.

Brie was supposed to listen to other speeches—from history, from sports—but she figured she'd get to that eventually. She could at least start her homework with these. What makes a good speech? Brie pulled out her English notebook and jotted down, *A good speech should be dramatic.*

Well, in soap operas, at least.

And while she had her backpack open and her notebook out, Brie figured she should consider doing her math problems and social studies questions, too. She was newly determined to be on top of her schoolwork, after all. But she decided one more scene before she started the rest of her homework wouldn't hurt. She pulled up another clip. It was a scene from *All My Children*. Brie recognized the character Erica Kane immediately—even people who didn't watch soaps knew Susan Lucci's iconic role—but she didn't recognize the other young woman. She hit Play.

"*This isn't me, Mom,*" said the young woman on Brie's computer screen, who was obviously Erica Kane's daughter. She was pretty and wearing a sparkly dress. "*It never was.*"

Brie leaned closer to the screen, already picturing herself repeating the lines in her mirror.

"*Well, all right, Bianca. Just tell me what look it is you're going for, and I'll have the stylists come up with something different.*" Bianca's mother had a voice just like Brie's mom. "*I mean, they're magicians—*"

"*No,*" Bianca interrupted, and Brie held her breath, waiting to see if Bianca could get her mother to listen. "*No, Mom.*"

" '*No, Mom' what?*"

There was a pause then. A long one.

"*I have to tell you something.*"

Brie stood up and crossed the room to close her bedroom door, glancing around first to see if anyone was nearby. Her mom and dad had not come out of their room.

"*Look at me!*" Bianca was yelling as Brie went back to the screen. "*I want you to see who I am, Mother. Can you see who I am? Can you? I'm trying to show you.*"

Brie lowered the volume a bit so she could hear if her parents came out into the hallway. She leaned in closer so she could also hear the conversation that was still happening on her computer.

"Bianca, what are you doing? What are you trying to say?"

Brie wanted Bianca's mom to just . . . *listen*. Was that really so hard? It was, it seemed, for Erica Kane, who had a press conference to get to and tears in her eyes as her daughter begged her to listen.

Brie was listening. She heard every word Bianca said.

Right up to the point where Bianca told her mother she was gay.

Brie stopped the video. Closed the tab. In the silence that followed she looked over at her closed bedroom door, listening to hear if anyone was in the hallway. Her face was hot; her hands sweaty. She tried to ignore those feelings. It was a stupid monologue, anyway. Not even a monologue. It was a conversation and it was useless to Brie, so she tried to forget it existed. She pulled up the transcript for the "Slut of Springfield" speech, pressed Print, and closed her laptop.

But try as she might, she couldn't stop thinking about the things Bianca had said and the way they made Brie's heart race. She pulled her laptop back open and started a new list:

ALL MY CHILDREN, December 2000:
Bianca tries to come out to her mom. Her mom does not listen . . .

6.

GUIDING LIGHT, July 1984:

Reva Shayne refuses to let Josh Lewis fling insults at her while he decides who he thinks she is. She takes matters—and those insults— into her own hands.

"I baptize myself the Slut of Springfield! Isn't that right, Joshua? Is that what you want?" screamed Brie from center stage in the school auditorium.

"You go on and call everybody out here!" she continued, focusing her anger on the front row of seats, where Ms. Brophy sat with Ms. Santos, who had volunteered to be the assistant director. Nico Han, a high schooler who had graduated from OLPH two years ago and had starred in *Alice in Wonderland* when Brie was in sixth grade, was also there. The three of them were in charge of casting. "Get them all out here! You have to come and watch me, the more the merrier! Joshua, isn't this fun? Don't you enjoy this? You look at me like I'm naked all the—"

"Okay! Thank you, Brie," Ms. Brophy loudly interrupted, her palms in the air. "That was very exuberant."

"In the scene, she's splashing around in a water fountain," Brie explained.

"Well, I'm grateful you took a drier approach. We've got all we need from you for today, so you're free to go if you have a parent here to pick you up. Otherwise, you're welcome to sit quietly in the back of the auditorium. We'll post the audition results outside the art room by next Friday," Ms. Brophy said.

Outside of the auditorium, Brie found Parker, who was pale—more so than usual, that is—and leaning against the hallway's white-painted cement wall.

"That was awesome!" Brie said.

"That was exhausting," Parker replied.

"I totally nailed it. I mean, I feel like I've been practicing for this for, like, ever," Brie said, taking a spot along the wall next to her best friend. "How'd you do? I'm sure you were fine. Besides, they'll cast everyone, you know? Like, plenty of ensemble roles and stuff."

"My mom told me to just look over their heads at the back wall, but I couldn't help it. I looked right at them. They were *staring* at me, Brie," Parker said.

Brie laughed. "That's kind of the point. That's the best part."

Parker emphatically shook her head.

"Just think about it!" Brie couldn't stop laughing. It was amazing how good she felt—and just because of the audition. The actual play would be *magic*. It had to be. "What if Jack or Wallace sits out in the audience? You'd be the center of their attention!"

"Oh *God*!"

Brie just kept laughing.

When her mom picked her up, Brie was in a more-than-good mood. "I think I did pretty good," she said. "Great, even!"

"Does Parker need a ride?" her mom asked. She waved to Parker, who was still sitting on the school's steps with Ms. Brophy and a few other kids waiting for their rides.

"No, Mrs. Pigott's coming. I don't think Parker did as good. She was kinda quiet and really nervous." Brie's mom pulled out of the school parking lot. Brie lowered her window. "But I'm pretty sure Ms. Brophy casts everyone, and I don't think Parker wants a real role anyway. But, Mom, guess what I used for my audition? You'll love it. I'm pretty sure I'm going to use it for my MCPA auditions, too."

"Brie," her mom said, pinching the bridge of her nose.

"I know, I know." Brie rolled her eyes. "You didn't exactly say yes yet."

Her mom didn't say anything, just kept her eyes on the road. Which concerned Brie, because usually her mom would be stating her opinion loudly by now. Her mom liked to yell at Brie for being dramatic, but really, she wasn't any better. Her mom stayed silent, her lips pressed tightly together. The tension building was worse than at the climax of a soap episode. Brie's stomach dropped when a voice in her head said, *What if Mom looked at your laptop?*

What if she saw Brie's Google search history or the scene between Erica Kane and Bianca she'd ended up bookmarking? What if her mom finally wanted to talk about those photos of Kelly Monaco she'd walked in on Brie looking at that day?

Brie would rather open the car door and leap into the street.

But then her mom took a deep breath and said, "We need to talk about your father."

Brie wasn't expecting that. "Trevor says he's depressed."

Her mom gripped the steering wheel tighter. She exhaled loudly through her nose before reaching for her Mary pendant. "Trevor needs to learn to keep his mouth shut."

Brie agreed, but did that mean Trevor was wrong? Or right?

"Your dad's not depressed. He's just . . . having a hard time. Losing his job was hard on him."

"I know," Brie said. "He told me. But I thought he liked working at the school?"

Her mom sighed again.

Brie blushed. Sometimes she felt like her mom's least favorite chore.

"We need to talk about that, too. He's only doing that for *you*, Gabrielle. So you could get the education we wanted for you and we wouldn't have to uproot you in eighth grade."

"I know that, too." They stopped at the red light nearest their house. If it had been green, they would have been home already. "What's going on? Why are you telling me this?"

"Things are going to change at home a bit. You know how I worked a lot more hours during the holidays?" her mom asked.

Brie nodded.

"I'm going to be picking those up again, working closer to full time. We need the extra income, and your dad needs . . . It'll just help lighten the load some if I do."

If Brie was being honest, she kind of liked the sound of that. Except . . .

"Will you be home for *General Hospital*?"

"Not all the time anymore, no."

Oh. Brie didn't like that. Not when they had been watching it together all this time. Brie thought it was special, thought it was the one thing they shared that couldn't be taken away.

Her mom, though, kept talking, not noticing the downward curve of Brie's mouth. "This means you're going to have to take more responsibility at home. I know you were looking forward to this spring play, but I'm not going to always be around to drive you to and from practices. Neither will your dad," her mom said.

"Trevor can—"

"The rules aren't changing. Trevor does not drive you."

"Parker's mom, then."

"It's not fair to put this all on Mrs. Pigott, either," her mom said. Brie started to argue, but her mom held up a hand. "I'll call her later and we'll discuss it. Point is, you have to learn to pull your weight. You haven't always, and quite frankly, Brie, I was nervous about your schoolwork up until lately. I'm glad that these auditions have you setting goals to work to your potential, and I was thrilled to hear you were chosen for the May Crowning. But you need to keep up that work. Your father is busting his butt. Do not take that for granted."

The light changed to green, but her mom was too focused on Brie to notice. The car behind them beeped. Her mom startled and pressed on the gas.

"I don't take it for granted," Brie said, her cheeks on fire.

"I think you do," her mom said. "You slack off at that school. And you sent away for that brochure without asking."

Brie clenched her jaw. "That's what this is really about. You said you'd think about it!"

"Your father will do everything he can to get you to that school. Do you even understand?" her mom asked.

Brie didn't understand the issue. "Yeah, I do! Why can't you do the same?"

They pulled into the driveway, and her mom put the car in park and turned off the engine. Neither one of them opened her door. "Your dad will do everything he can, no matter what that means for him. You're asking too much. I need you to start thinking about *that*."

It was all Brie could think about, really. Because she *was* working hard, wasn't she? Brie wanted this. Why would her dad work at the school so she could keep going to OLPH if they didn't want her to reach for her dreams? Didn't she owe it to him to at least try? Wasn't that the point?

Or was the point to keep Brie in a place where she was made to pray three times a day, attend mass once a week, and take daily religion classes where Sister Patricia went on and on about things Brie had literally heard over and over again every Sunday since she'd been born. Which would make her mom the selfish one, not Brie. Right? Because her mom wanted them to pray and go to church, even though Brie could go to public school for free. That would allow her dad to rest, and she could get him to drive her to play rehearsal because he'd be home anyway.

Brie didn't need to sit in religion class, like she was today, while Sister Patricia droned on and on about confirmation.

She could do all this Catholic stuff *just fine* while going to public school with after-school CCD classes.

Why did her mom care so much about all of this, anyway?

Brie, obviously, wasn't a fan of religion class. It was basically an extension of church, only with textbooks. Kids who looked exceptionally pleased with themselves for spreading the good word of the Lord smiled up at her from every page. Brie drew glasses and mustaches on most of them.

She was coloring in the teeth of a super-happy boy so that he looked like he had none, when Sister Patricia tapped Brie's desk to get her attention. "I know the focus always ends up on the May Crowning, but confirmation is quite frankly more important, and I'd like you all to really start preparing," Sister Patricia said. She was an older woman with a face so round it resembled the moon. Her eyebrows and eyelashes were so light, from a distance it looked like she didn't have any. She wore her hair tucked up under her blue habit, so for all Brie knew, she could have been bald.

She'd asked about it once, back in fifth grade, but Sister Patricia had scolded her for being rude. She hadn't asked Sister Patricia any more questions after that.

Sister Patricia turned to the chalkboard and started writing. She was the only one of their teachers who still used chalk instead of whiteboard markers. "We need to really think about faith and, particularly, why it's important to you. The point of confirmation is to strengthen your relationship with God. It's the completion of baptism: it's *you* deciding to continue this journey."

Well, that didn't exactly sound right. Brie wasn't sure there was any real decision-making in it, particularly when there was a grade attached to her participation.

Whatever, Brie thought. The sacrament of confirmation would come and go no matter what Brie decided about it in the interim. The May Crowning might not be as important to Sister Patricia, but for Brie it had much bigger stakes, and she wished Sister Patricia would talk more about *that* instead. Especially because Brie could learn how to write an award-winning essay all she wanted, but that ability wouldn't mean anything if she didn't know squat about the subject. She needed Sister Patricia to teach her more about *Mary*.

When the bell rang and everyone gathered their belongings to head back to their homerooms for dismissal, Sister Patricia headed toward the main office to do the end-of-the-day prayers. Brie followed her. "Sister Patricia? I have some questions."

"You should have asked in class. I need to go make the dismissal announcements." Luckily, Sister Patricia walked slowly. It would take some time before they reached the office.

So Brie asked her questions anyway. Because she sure as heck wasn't about to ask in front of all her classmates. "My mom loves Mary. I mean, like, *loves* her. Like, she wears this pendant around her neck that has Mary on it that she rubs all the time instead of just praying. And, I mean, we do this whole thing in May, and I get it—I do. It's a huge deal that she was the Mother of God. I know that."

"Is there a question coming, Gabrielle?" They reached the small set of stairs that led up to the hallway outside the main office, and Sister Patricia placed a hand on Brie's shoulder to steady herself for the climb. Brie reached for Sister Patricia's hand for extra support.

"I've been thinking about my May Crowning essay. I want to do a good job. It's just hard. I don't feel like my mom does, I don't think. Sometimes everything feels so . . ." Brie hesitated, because should she really be admitting this to a *nun*, of all people?

"A lot of people your age have trouble finding and understanding their faith. You have technology at your fingertips, Google to give you all the answers." They reached the main-office doors, but Sister Patricia didn't immediately go in. "It's harder when it's something you can't Google, I'd imagine. You feel a little disconnected?"

Brie nodded. "Yeah. That."

"Have you tried asking your mother to explain why she feels the way she does?" Sister Patricia asked.

Brie almost laughed. *Yeah right*.

"You're exceptionally late to homeroom. You'd better get going," Sister Patricia said as she opened the main-office door.

"But wait, I—"

"Mary is the Mother of God," Sister Patricia said. "So if you really want somewhere to start? I suggest you start with your own."

Brie thought about asking her mom. She really did.

She sat with her mom during *General Hospital*, trying to figure out exactly how to start the conversation every time the show went to commercial. It should have been easy, especially since her mom's pendant hung shining against her blouse, right out in the open for Brie to mention. But her stomach kind of hurt, and she couldn't find the words, and during what she knew had to be the last commercial break, instead of opening her mouth, she went to the bathroom.

It shouldn't have shocked her. She'd been there when Deena Yousef got her period in gym class last year. And Parker had been getting hers since the sixth grade. If anything, she should have been extra prepared, since she was on the later side and knew it would eventually happen. Now she had to go ask her mom for help, because she wasn't prepared, she didn't have supplies, and this was kind of gross and awkward. But if she couldn't even ask her mom about Mary, how on earth was she supposed to talk to her about this?

She couldn't. And she couldn't really explain why, because it was so normal, and her mom must have been expecting it soon, too. But Brie felt funny, and instead she bunched up toilet paper to put into her underpants and went back out into the living room. She sat down on the couch to finish watching *General Hospital*, and when her mom said, "I'm glad they recast him. He's much cuter," Brie simply responded, "Yeah."

It was hours later, when she was getting ready for bed and her mom came in to say good night, that Brie finally said, "Mom? I think . . . I mean, I got my period."

Her mom blinked at her for a moment. "When? Why didn't you say anything?"

Brie didn't have a real answer for that.

She should have been relieved—even if she was crampy—when she was all situated and ready to go to bed. She couldn't sleep, though. Not when she kept thinking that she barely knew how to navigate her relationship with her own mother. How on earth was she supposed to figure out one with Mary?

March

Ten Sundays until
the May Crowning

7.

AS THE WORLD TURNS, May 2006:
Luke Snyder comes out as gay. It is very
dramatic. It does not go well. His dad wants to fix
him. His mom says he's too young and confused.
I, Brie Hutchens, hate all of it.

The chapel was always hot and stuffy when the whole school
attended church together, which happened precisely once a
week. At least twice during the school year, someone passed
out. It was so commonplace, the priest barely stopped his
sermon when it happened.

It was a gloomy sort of spring day, and the chapel was
dim. The colors in the stained-glass windows were muted
without the sunlight bursting through them. Brie was sand-
wiched between Wallace (as usual) and Chris Iasparro (who

always wore the puffiest coat, which took up half the pew, even though it was hot and cramped already). Luckily, Parker ended up in the pew right behind her, so Brie could lean back and whisper with her.

They all stood as Father Dave, with hands raised toward the sky, started reading. He was one of their younger priests, with a full beard and a big smile. Next to him, Kennedy, dressed in white robes, held up the Bible he was reading from. Kennedy was an altar server, because of course she was.

Brie barely watched Father Dave. A strand of Kennedy's dark hair was out of place, falling on the wrong side of her part. Brie wanted to fix it.

Without thinking, she leaned back to whisper to Parker, "Do you ever just really like the way another girl's face looks?"

Parker's entire face scrunched up. "What?"

Brie took that as a no and slumped back in the pew. Parker noticed boys. Parker *always* noticed boys. She noticed Jack Thomas's birthmark and Javi Martinez's rolled shirtsleeves and Shaun Frankel's funny—but cute, according to Parker—snaggletooth.

Parker did not notice the way Kennedy always had a loose and dangling strand of hair falling over her face or that three freckles dotted her nose.

"I like the way Deena's eyes are always squinty when she looks at the blackboard," Wallace chimed in. "Does that count?"

"Deena probably needs glasses," Brie said. "So no, I don't think that counts."

Wallace tilted his head to the side. "I still think I like it."

Brie rolled her eyes and fought the urge to shout to Parker, *See! Wallace gets it! Why can't you?* But Brie knew the answer.

Up on the altar, Kennedy took her seat, reaching up to tuck the stray hair behind her ear.

$$*$$

After mass, the students lined up in rows of girls and boys and marched back down the hallways to homeroom. Parker, who was in front of Brie, tugged at the bottom of her skirt hem. It had bunched up from all the sitting and standing and looked short enough to get her in trouble. Though with her long legs, Parker's skirt almost always looked too short.

As Brie approached her homeroom, instead of following her classmates, she kept walking. (She had found that if you walked like you were supposed to be somewhere, no one really questioned it.) It was chillier in the building than it was outside, the cool March air getting trapped in the concrete hallways. Brie buttoned her sweater to the top, even though no one really ever wore them that way.

Brie beat Ms. Brophy to her office, meaning she was going to be really late to homeroom. She might even be late to her first class, since every period—including homeroom—was shortened on the mornings they had mass. But

Brie couldn't wait an entire school day. She *had* to see that cast list, which Ms. Brophy had promised would be hanging up outside her office on Friday.

Well, it was Friday. And the wall space outside Ms. Brophy's office was bare.

"Oh, Brie! You startled me!" Ms. Brophy said as she turned the corner. She was carrying a briefcase, a large box filled with paper and paint bottles, and a few folders. She also apparently shopped at the same puffy-coat store as Chris Iasparro. Ms. Brophy looked like she was going to drop all her belongings. "Shouldn't you be in homeroom?" she asked as she reached to unlock her office door. Brie took the keys and unlocked the door for her.

"I was hoping you'd be here to put up the cast list," Brie said.

"Top folder. No, wait, the blue one. Bottom folder," Ms. Brophy said, gesturing with her body to the folders on top of the box in her arms. "Should be the first paper in there. Tape it to the door for me, will you?"

Brie reached for the folder (almost knocking everything else Ms. Brophy was carrying out of her arms in the process) and quickly opened it.

She looked for her name, scrolling down, and down, and down the paper, her eyebrows creasing more and more with each name she passed.

Then she found it. "I'm *Grumpy*?"

Brie was pouting. Parker knew she was pouting; Wallace knew she was pouting. Anyone who walked by them during recess knew she was pouting.

"You can take my part instead," Parker said. She had been paler than usual (which was quite a feat) ever since she had seen her name on the top of the cast list.

Brie groaned. "No, you earned it."

"Congrats, by the way," Wallace added.

Parker turned from pale to pink within seconds.

"And at least it's a part, Brie," Wallace continued. "I mean, it's not like you're sitting on the bench. You're still playing the game with the rest of the team."

"Don't talk sports metaphors at me, Wallace. I'm not in the mood."

"Jeez, no wonder she cast you as Grumpy."

The three of them were on the swings. Wallace twisted the chains around so he went spinning, and Parker let the wind blow her gently back and forth, dragging her feet. Brie was leaning back, her head nearly touching the ground as she stared at the sky. It was chilly out, but the students had been restless inside, so the faculty bundled them up for recess.

"Can I take this swing?"

The voice startled Brie, who tried to sit up in her own swing too quickly and instead fell off it and onto her face. Wallace laughed hysterically as Brie looked up to meet Kennedy's gaze. She hovered by Brie's abandoned swing. "Are you okay?" she asked.

"Peachy," Brie said, fixing her skirt as she stood. Her stockings had a new tear. Her mom would be thrilled. She sat back on her swing and gestured to the open one. "Swing's all yours."

Kennedy took a seat and started swinging. "I heard you and Parker made the school play. That's so cool."

Brie blushed. "I'm just a dwarf. Parker's got a lead."

"I'm the old hag!" Parker said.

"The Evil Queen! You give Snow White the poison apple, *and* you have a ton of lines. That's huge!" Brie responded, shaking her head. "My mom is going to give me so much crap about this."

"How come?" Kennedy asked.

"To answer that, I would have to explain my mother, and that would take more time than we've got left in recess," Brie said.

"SparkNotes: Brie's mom doesn't want her attending MCPA next year," Parker supplied. "The spring play was supposed to help."

"As is crowning Mary," Wallace added.

"Thank you. What would I do without you?" Brie scowled at the two of them.

Kennedy was smiling.

"What?" Brie asked her.

"Nothing, I just . . ." She shook her head. "What's the May Crowning have to do with performing arts school?"

Nothing and everything. The seventh-grade teacher on recess duty began ringing the bell, letting them know time was up. The four of them stood from their swings.

"My mom really wants me to crown Mary, too," Kennedy said before turning to head back inside.

Wallace whistled. "Told you," he whispered. "Someone like Kennedy is gonna crown Mary."

Brie clenched her jaw. "Not if I write a better essay."

"How are you going to do that?" Wallace asked.

Brie watched as Kennedy walked ahead of them, the first in the eighth-grade line. Kennedy took off one of her gloves to tuck her hair behind her ear, like she always did.

Wallace had a point. Kennedy was one of the best students in their class, and if Kennedy's mom wanted her to crown Mary, Kennedy would do the work, would be the best (like always), and would crown Mary.

Brie needed Kennedy's help if she was going to stand a chance. "Hey, Kennedy!" she shouted and waited for Kennedy to turn around. "Do you want to come over after school?"

It was strange to have Kennedy Bishop in her bedroom. Brie kind of wished she had at least made her bed that morning.

Brie was perched awkwardly on a pile of crumpled blankets on her bed. Kennedy sat in her desk chair. They had both abandoned their school skirts for sweatpants. Brie had also abandoned her sweater, though Kennedy had just unbuttoned hers.

Kennedy looked around and reached for the magazines next to Brie's laptop. "*Soaps in Depth*?" she asked.

Brie felt her neck grow warm. "Uh, yeah. I, uh. I like soap operas. *Soap Opera Digest* is in there, too."

Kennedy flipped through the pages of *Soaps in Depth*. Brie squirmed in her seat before abruptly getting up to place her hand on the magazine and stop Kennedy from looking further.

"I've never watched a soap opera before," Kennedy said. "Honestly, I've never known anyone our age who did."

"Do your parents work during the day?"

"Yeah."

"My mom works part-time, but she used to be home in the afternoons. So we watched them a *lot*. She loves them. I do, too."

Kennedy smiled. "It's nice that you share that."

"Yeah, I guess. Look, what speech are you using for Ms. Santos?" Brie reached for her laptop. She leaned over Kennedy as she pulled it open and went into her bookmarks. Their English assignment for the week was to choose one speech and analyze the techniques used throughout it. "I have like fifteen of them saved. I can't decide on a good one. Parker's got an Obama speech, and Wallace took one from a sports movie. I can't find one I like, and Ms. Santos keeps asking me how I'm doing."

"My mom helped me pick a speech by Susan B. Anthony about women's suffrage," Kennedy said. "It was pretty cool."

"I saw that one," Brie said, clicking on one of her bookmarks. "This it?"

Kennedy nodded. "My mom and I went to a women's march a couple years ago, and I loved it. It sort of made me realize I want to go into politics someday."

"With a name like Kennedy . . ."

She laughed. "Yeah. But I really want to help push women's rights, so I thought this would be a good speech to analyze, you know?"

Brie closed the tab. "See, that's the thing. You've got your women's speech, and Wallace has his hockey speech. Of *course* you guys are going to do a good job with it. You actually enjoy it."

"So why don't you try and look for something you'll enjoy?" Kennedy said. "What *do* you enjoy, Brie?"

Brie looked around her room—at the fake Daytime Emmy Award her brother had gotten her for her birthday last year, the soap opera magazines, and the background picture on her laptop of soap opera power couple Jason Morgan and Sam McCall (played by Kelly Monaco—fully clothed). She even had, tucked into the corner of her bedroom mirror, all the playbills from the MCPA shows she and her mom had gone to over the years.

She slumped her shoulders. "I like soaps. I like acting."

Kennedy pulled the laptop closer to her and started typing. Her hair slipped out from behind her ear and brushed against Brie's cheek for a moment, until Brie pushed away from the desk, where she'd been leaning—a bit too close to Kennedy—and stood ramrod straight.

"Well, have you tried looking up a famous soap opera speech?" Kennedy asked.

Brie's shoulders tensed as she thought about the document she had been adding more and more soap scenes to ever since she'd watched the one with Bianca. "I don't think that's helpful—"

But Kennedy had already hit the search button, and the first link that came up was *the* scene. The one with Bianca and her mom. The link was purple, instead of blue, and Brie wondered if Kennedy noticed, if Kennedy realized Brie had already clicked that link, had already watched that video and bookmarked it.

Brie didn't wait to find out. She closed her laptop quickly and looked up at Kennedy, who turned to stare at her, confused, as Brie picked up the laptop and chucked it onto her bed. "You know what? I changed my mind. I don't want to talk about schoolwork."

"What do you want to talk about, then?" Kennedy asked. Her voice was quiet and soft, and Brie stayed close, even though the laptop wasn't between them anymore and she had no reason to

Brie's mouth went dry, and all she could think about was how she'd never known what color Kennedy's eyes were until that moment. They weren't just brown; they were brown and green and gray, and Brie couldn't stop looking at them or at the three freckles on Kennedy's nose as Brie leaned closer.

"What do you think is so special about faith?" Brie suddenly found herself saying. She was practically sweating and tried to backtrack. "I mean, with the May Crowning essay. Do you even know what you'd write?"

"Well, I'd write about Mary."

"No, I know," Brie said. "But I mean . . . I don't know what I mean. It's like . . . I know we literally pray every morning and before dismissal, and we go to mass every Friday—and then my mom drags us again every Sunday. We sit in religion class and study the Bible or whatever, and we have confirmation soon, and I just . . . still feel so . . ." She waved her hand in front of her, creating an invisible wall. "Separated from it, I guess."

Kennedy nodded, and Brie felt like she really meant that nod, like someone was actually following along for once. "I understand. Really. I think . . ."

"What?" Brie asked, practically whispering, still standing too close, still looking at Kennedy's eyes.

"Sometimes it's easier to keep it at a distance, I guess. Religion, I mean," Kennedy said. "Like, having that protection . . . to keep from getting hurt."

Brie realized she was holding her breath. "Getting hurt from what?"

Kennedy paused, her eyes drifting to the side as she thought about it.

But she thought a little too long, because at that moment Brie's mother barged through her bedroom door without knocking. Brie practically leaped away from Kennedy to fall back onto her bed.

"Brie, dinner will be ready in a half hour, so have Kennedy call her mom soon," her mom said, brow creased as she watched Brie regain her balance. "You two okay in here?"

"Yes, Mom!" Brie said, a little too cheerfully, a little too loudly.

Her mom paused for a beat. "All right," she said and left without closing the door.

Brie was certain anyone could see her pulse fluttering quickly in her neck and her chest. Her arms and legs felt tingly.

She had a hard time looking back at Kennedy's brown-green-gray eyes. "You should call your mom," she mumbled.

Kennedy hesitated for a moment but turned away to reach for her cell phone in her backpack. With Kennedy's back turned, Brie was able to breathe again.

That evening, Brie stayed downstairs after dinner instead of vacating to her room like usual, wondering why she felt like she should be in trouble and why she felt so . . . sweaty about Kennedy's visit. She sat on the living room couch while her mom and dad watched the news. Normally she'd be on YouTube now, watching soap clips as Parker texted her about Wallace and Jack Thomas and Javi Martinez and all the other boys she'd crushed on today, instead of sitting with her parents while she texted Parker.

I think I like Wallace and Javi as friends but Jack as a boyfriend, Parker texted. *Did Kennedy help with your homework?*

Brie hovered her fingers over the screen. *Kennedy likes politics and I think I like Kennedy*, Brie typed. *But not like we like Wallace, more like you like Jack.*

Brie did not hit Send.

8.

GENERAL HOSPITAL, March 2016:
Kristina Davis has a fling with another woman.
She comes out to her mom. She comes out to her
sisters. She comes out to her dad. She comes
out again and again and again. It all seems very
exhausting.

Snow White rehearsals started the following week. They took place in the school's auditorium, which was also the school's gym and where they held a lot of parish masses. The chapel was too small to hold the entire congregation, so the stage—where they would perform their play—doubled as an altar on the weekends.

That's where Brie sat, in the center of the stage, surrounded by everyone else who'd auditioned, boxes of Communion wafers, crucifixes, and the big green plants they used to decorate the altar. Ms. Brophy stood below them, on the floor in front of the stage.

"Welcome, welcome!" she bellowed. "I hope you all took the time to research the parts you have been given, but we'll get to those in a bit." Ms. Brophy motioned to her side, nearly hitting Ms. Santos in the face with the papers in her hands. Nico Han stood a safe distance away, probably from experience. "Ms. Santos was kind enough to volunteer to help assistant direct, and I'm sure a lot of you remember Nico. She had the leading role her eighth-grade year and has agreed to help. I expect you to give both of them your full respect."

There were murmurs of agreement from everyone onstage, and Ms. Brophy continued to ramble on about rehearsal times and how important showing up to practice was—especially for the leads. Brie was not a lead. She looked around at the rest of the cast. There was Jack Thomas—which Parker was pleased about—along with Shaun Frankel and Anthony Esposito. Deena Yousef was playing *Snow White* and was now Brie's public enemy number one.

She was glad she'd convinced Parker to do the play, because the whole ordeal made Brie feel like she had a dark cloud over her head. Her mom was on her case about how much time rehearsals were going to take up—and how much Brie was going to have to depend on Parker's mom to drive her to and from them—and Brie still hadn't told her she was only a dwarf. All that time repeating lines in front of the mirror. All that time watching soaps, daydreaming about the day her mom would get to sit and *watch* her, instead of sit with her. Brie really thought she was better than Grumpy.

The doors in the back of the auditorium swung open, and Brie was surprised to see her dad walk in. His face lit up and he waved at her, and Brie gave him a small smile as she pulled her knees into her chest. She figured maybe he had to set up the chairs on the basketball court for mass or an assembly, but then Ms. Brophy said, "Oh good! He's here."

Brie's eyebrows must have disappeared into her hairline. Her palms started sweating the moment Ms. Brophy looked over at her. "Brie! Why don't you introduce everyone to your dad?"

Everyone turned to look at her. Brie tried to keep the smile on her face. Her dad had been working at their school since September, and it was now March. They had all seen him in the halls and on the playground and not once had Brie mentioned she knew who he was.

"He's your *dad*?" Shaun didn't quite stage-whisper.

When Brie said nothing, Ms. Brophy took the lead, wrapping an arm around Brie's father when he approached her. "This is Mr. Hutchens. He's volunteered to make our sets."

He had his hands buried in his jean pockets and was wearing the flannel top that Brie's mom hated. His gray hair was messy on the top of his head. He always ran his fingers through it, just like Kennedy did, except his didn't fall back as neatly. "Hi, everyone," he said in a small voice.

His eyes met Brie's. She looked down at her shoes.

$$\ast$$

"I just don't understand why he didn't tell me," Brie said, leaning against the kitchen counter as her mom prepared dinner.

"He doesn't know how to talk to you," her mom replied. "Wash your hands so I can show you how to make this."

Brie pushed herself off the counter and walked over to the sink. "That's not fair. I actually *like* talking to Dad."

"What's that supposed to mean?"

Brie quickly washed her hands, rolled her eyes, and reached for the paper towels. "*Nothing*, I'm just saying. We talk all the time."

Her mom handed her a bag of green beans. "Take the tips off of these."

"Why?" Brie asked as her mom pushed the garbage can closer to her.

"Because the ends are tough."

Brie touched the tip of one. "Doesn't feel so tough."

"Gabrielle, just do it, please."

Brie pulled a handful of green beans out of the bag and lined them up to rip off a bunch of tips at once. Her mom was showing Brie how to prepare a bunch of easy meals, since she was going to start working more night shifts, and God forbid Trevor learned how to do anything useful. "Well, I wish Dad asked me first, at least."

"I don't understand what the big deal is," her mom said as she sprayed a pan with cooking oil. "If he's doing work for your play, he'll be able to drive you home some days, which will be a big help."

"I didn't tell anyone he was my dad," Brie said.

Her mom turned to look at her, eyebrows scrunched together. "He's been working at your school since September. You don't see him in the halls?"

Brie tried to focus on the green beans and not on the look on her mom's face. "I do."

Her mom sighed but didn't say anything more.

Brie felt as though she was in trouble anyway. "I mean, Parker knows, obviously. It just . . . doesn't come up, is all. It's not like we can talk to each other. He's working. I'm, you know, *learning*."

"There's nothing embarrassing about doing custodial work," her mom said, using one hand to pass a bowl to Brie to put the green beans in and toying with her pendant with the other hand. "Even if he didn't have to do it so you can keep going to school there—which he does, I'll remind you—there's nothing wrong with doing that kind of work. I don't want you being the type of person who thinks there is."

"I don't, Mom. That's not it at all."

"Then what is it?"

"It's just . . . it's *Dad*."

"So it's your dad that embarrasses you, not the job. That's real nice, Brie."

This conversation was getting away from her. She threw the bag of green beans on the counter. "No! That's not what I said. You always do this. I'm not embarrassed of Dad—I just don't like that he's at my school!"

"I, uh, can ask Diane Brophy if someone else can do the sets if you want, Brie," her dad's voice suddenly rang out.

Brie didn't realize he was even downstairs, let alone near the kitchen.

He leaned against the wall, hands in his pockets, and shrugged. "I don't want to make middle school any harder for you than it needs to be."

"No, don't do that. You're fine," Brie's mom said, her face softening as she looked at Brie's dad. "And you made a commitment. Both of you made a commitment. Right, Brie? Tell your father it's fine."

Looking at her dad, Brie felt more chastised than she had when her mom had been arguing with her. "It's okay, Dad."

He smiled, but it didn't look quite right.

$$\ast$$

That night, there was yet another hockey game. Brie didn't know how she kept ending up committing to these things, but there she was. And she had to admit she was glad to get out of the house. It was hard to know where to focus her gaze when she couldn't bring herself to look into her dad's tired, droopy eyes while he sat around at home with nothing to do.

The other good thing about that night's hockey game was that MCPA was selling tickets to their big spring play in the main foyer of the ice rink. Brie's mom had given her money to buy them two tickets—after a bit of reminding and prodding during dinner from Brie—just like she did every year. Two high school students in full costume sat at a table. A big sign painted with MUCH ADO ABOUT NOTHING hung behind them.

"I don't think I like Shakespeare," Brie said to Parker as they stood in line.

"You'll like this one," one of the students behind the table said.

At least it wasn't *Romeo and Juliet*. Brie *knew* she didn't like that one.

After Brie got her tickets, she and Parker found their seats. Wallace and Jack were both already on the ice, as was a boy on the other team who caught Parker's eye.

"Oh, he's cute!"

Brie sometimes couldn't keep up, but it was all so very *Parker*, she didn't mind. That is, until Parker added, "What about you, Brie? There *has* to be someone you crush on by now."

At that very moment, Kennedy and her family decided to walk in. Their timing was flawless.

"Boys are exhausting," Brie said. "Even Wallace is exhausting, and he's just a friend."

Parker tilted her head to the side, considering this. "Am I exhausting?" she asked.

Brie laughed. "Oh yes."

Parker shoved her, both of them erupting in giggles, as Kennedy's family sat in the row of bleachers right in front of them. Brie held up her hand in a wave that lasted a little too long. Still, Kennedy returned it. She sat right in front of Brie, close enough that Kennedy's back was pretty much leaning against Brie's knees. Brie opened her legs wider so that they surrounded Kennedy instead of supporting her, but then she decided that was worse and closed them again.

"Did you hear what happened to Shaun?" Parker suddenly asked.

"No, what?" Brie asked, noticing that Kennedy turned around to listen, too, her long dark hair static-clinging to Brie's jeans.

"He got in-school suspension," Parker told them. "I was at the office today when he was waiting for his mom to pick him up, because Mrs. Dwek asked me to hand in the lunch order."

"What'd he do?" Brie asked. "Shaun's annoying, but they can't suspend him for that."

Parker leaned in, her eyes wide in a way that told Brie she was about to tell them something good. Brie leaned in, too, and Kennedy followed. "He got caught on his phone at recess."

85

"So?" Brie said. "Everyone uses their phones at recess."

"Shh! I'm not done!" Parker said. She was just as dramatic as Brie sometimes. "Apparently he was looking at . . ." Parker glanced around, then dropped her voice to even more of a whisper. "*Boy-boy* stuff. You know, like, two guys kissing and *stuff*."

"What?" Kennedy said, eyes wide. She looked over at her parents to check if they were listening.

"Oh God." Brie's laughter was small and wobbly. "Did they send him to talk to Father Dave?"

Parker shrugged. "I'm not sure. I just know he was waiting outside the office for his mom to pick him up."

Kennedy, eyes still popping out of her head, quickly checked on her parents again. The game had begun, and luckily, most people were focused on the ice.

Brie, chest tight, lowered her voice when she asked, "Is Shaun gay?"

Parker shrugged. "Chris said Shaun and Javi were just messing around on his phone."

Someone scored. Brie wasn't even sure which team it was. There were cheers and groans all around her, and even Parker focused her attention on the hockey game.

In front of her, Kennedy had turned back around.

Brie wanted to talk to Parker about it, about how maybe Shaun or Javi (or both) hadn't just been messing around. About how Brie sometimes Googled things, too. About how she had an entire Google Doc of . . . of gay soap opera scenes, of *coming-out* scenes, that she had compiled while searching.

But she didn't know how. Parker liked boys. Parker *loved* boys. Parker—if their conversation in the chapel was any indication—had never looked at another girl and noticed her smile or thought how pretty her hair was. Maybe Parker would giggle over girl *or* boy crushes with Brie—maybe it didn't matter—but Brie didn't know how to find out

And what if Brie was wrong? What if the flutter she felt in her stomach when she saw Kennedy, and the way her gut twisted during soap opera scenes, didn't mean anything? What if there was still a boy out there who didn't go to OLPH that maybe Brie could like? What if she told Parker things she couldn't take back? If she said the words out loud . . . if she told Parker . . . that would make it all real, wouldn't it? The things she was feeling and trying to sort out—if she said those words out loud, if she actually told someone . . . then they would be *real*. Then they would be *true*.

Brie wasn't ready for that.

And then there was still the issue of her mother. Her mom, who already wished Brie were smarter, more responsible, and more like Kennedy, without even considering that her daughter might have crushes on girls. Her mom, who went to church and grasped her Mary pendant, listened to the priest's sermon, and read Bible passages. Her mom, who wasn't disconnected from religion and faith, who listened to and took in and understood all the things that had made Brie start tuning out during mass and religion class in the first place.

Even if a miracle happened and Brie got to crown Mary, she still couldn't change this. She would still be the girl who Googled pictures of Kelly Monaco and *liked* it. Whether her mom found out now or much later, the end result would be the same.

The buzzer sounded, and Brie jumped. Parker was clapping wildly beside her, so Brie assumed it was their team who'd scored, but she couldn't bring herself to care. She didn't even have it in her to pretend to.

9.

THE YOUNG AND THE RESTLESS, November 2017: Mariah Copeland explains how she feels to her mom. How she doesn't feel strongly about the boy she's seeing. How she's never felt strongly about any of the boys she's dated. Her mom tells her there are other boys out there. Mariah tells her she's already found someone . . . and that someone is a she.

Come Monday, Brie couldn't shake those thoughts of eventually telling Parker, of eventually telling her mom, of how terrifying it felt to just . . . *say* it and make it real . . . particularly when Shaun didn't show up to class. He was stuck in the office for his suspension.

Brie sat in English class with her nose burning as she held in possible tears and her jaw clenched, watching Kennedy raise her hand again and again as Ms. Santos asked questions. "What's the central question the author is trying to ask and answer in this essay?" Ms. Santos asked.

Brie hesitantly raised her hand.

Kennedy raised hers higher.

"Brie." Ms. Santos called on her. "What do you think?"

"Um," Brie said. "Friendship? Because she says how her friends end up being most important."

Ms. Santos's smile was soft and kind. "Very good start. Anyone else have an idea?"

Very good start. As in, *Nice try, but not quite.* As in, *You are wrong, Brie Hutchens.*

Kennedy, hand raised yet again, knew the correct answer, of course.

Brie's mom really *would* like Kennedy. Or at least, she would until she realized how Brie might *really* like her. Kennedy's hair was pulled into a high ponytail, and it swayed every time she moved, every time she raised her hand with the right answer. Brie didn't want to notice that. She didn't want to notice how the back of Kennedy's uniform shirt had come untucked, and she didn't want to feel disappointed that with her hair pulled back, Kennedy didn't have anything to tuck behind her ears.

Brie didn't want to notice Kennedy. And Kennedy was making it harder and harder since she kept drawing attention to herself. Why did she have to make things so complicated?

Ms. Santos asked, "Okay, Kennedy, what do you think the theme is?"

Brie's chest was too tight.

"Let someone else get it right for once, Kennedy!" she shouted. In the silence that followed, Brie could hear her pulse in her ears.

She sank down in her seat. The rest of the class and Ms. Santos stared at her.

"Brie, I'd like you to hang back after class for a bit," Ms. Santos said.

Brie didn't argue. She nodded, rested her chin on her desk, and ignored the questions written all over Parker's face. When Brie's eyes found Kennedy, she noticed Kennedy was beet red and looking directly at the floor.

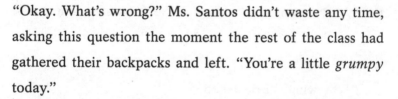

"Okay. What's wrong?" Ms. Santos didn't waste any time, asking this question the moment the rest of the class had gathered their backpacks and left. "You're a little *grumpy* today."

Ms. Santos laughed at her own joke, but Brie shot her a side-eyed look. She wasn't really in the mood to think about *all* her shortcomings at once. "Just tired. Sorry." It sounded like a good excuse. It was a well-worn one in her house lately.

Ms. Santos reached down and opened the bottom drawer of her desk, pulling out a stack of papers Brie recognized as the essays they had read and analyzed earlier that week. She thumbed through the pages until she came across Brie's name. "Here. Check this out."

Brie took the essay. She noticed the red markings throughout were sparse. Noticed the grade on the top was . . . "An *A*? I got an A?"

"That right there is the best grade you've gotten in my class all year," Ms. Santos said. "I was grading these in the faculty lounge during recess the other day, and Sister Patricia said your grades went up in her class, too." Ms. Santos paused. "Mrs. Dwek's class, not so much."

"I hate math," Brie said.

"You didn't seem to like English much, either, until recently."

Brie pulled a face. "I didn't say I like it now."

Ms. Santos laughed and returned Brie's essay to the stack. "My point is, it's okay to be frustrated, but you're working hard, and it shows. I guess I'm just curious as to, well . . . *why*."

"Why what?" Brie asked.

"Why one of my more unmotivated students is suddenly extremely motivated, over halfway through the school year." Ms. Santos's face grew more serious. "To the point where she's taking it out on other students."

Brie sighed and hung her head. She didn't want to be having this conversation, especially when Parker and Wallace and all her other classmates were free to enjoy their lunch period, which was currently ticking away. Brie glanced at the clock.

"Hey, come on. You can talk to me, Brie. What's going on?"

Could she talk to Ms. Santos? It wasn't like she had anyone else. She didn't know how to talk to Parker, and she couldn't and *wouldn't* talk to her mom.

But she was also already flushed and sweaty from just having Ms. Santos's attention, in a way that, well, Brie *knew* Parker wouldn't understand. And maybe Ms. Santos wouldn't, either.

"If it really is just frustration that got to you today, well, you're not always going to learn the material immediately, no matter how hard you try," Ms. Santos continued. "Change takes time."

"But change can happen? You can help me make it happen?" Brie found herself asking.

Ms. Santos pressed her lips together in consideration. "I'm here to help you. If you get stuck or upset like that again, just talk to me. We can work out any hiccups. If you want to learn, I want to help you do that."

Which was all very nice and well, but not the point. "What about . . . feelings?" Brie asked, her voice lowering even though the room was still empty. "Can they change, too?"

Ms. Santos, with an upturn of her lips and brightness in her eyes, said, "Now that's an entirely different conversation altogether. Unfortunately, I am absolutely not an expert on feelings."

Brie sighed. "Can I go now, then?"

"Yeah, okay. But Brie, before you go . . . just know that whatever you're feeling? These things you want to change?" Ms. Santos said. "I'm positive you're not alone. It may suck, but as cliché as it is to say, you're at the age where feelings get confusing. It's completely normal, whatever it is."

Brie decided right then and there that teachers did *not* know everything.

10.

ALL MY CHILDREN, February 2009:
Bianca marries Reese Williams. I thought it would
make me feel better to see that Bianca gets to
be happy. I don't know why it just makes my
stomach hurt.

Brie ignored all the texts she got from Parker and Wallace
after school. She didn't want to talk to anyone, didn't want
anyone talking to her. The tightness in her chest was still
there—it might have even been worse—and she was grateful when she saw the note on the kitchen table that said her
mom had picked up an extra shift at work.

Her dad had gone to get groceries, and Trevor's car
wasn't in the driveway. Brie was home alone. She dropped
her backpack unceremoniously on the ground, kicked off her
shoes, and ran up the stairs, slamming her door closed in a

way that would have gotten her in big trouble if her mom had been there. She took off her skirt—which always felt a little too tight, even on a good day, because she rolled it shorter—and was able to breathe a little easier as she opened up her laptop.

She pulled up Google Docs and YouTube. Her phone buzzed again, but she continued to ignore it. Her hands were cold but sweaty as she placed them on the keyboard and typed *LGBTQ soap opera scenes.*

Maybe it happened because the tightness in Brie's chest seemed to loosen as she let the first scene play, and then the next one, and then the next one, until she got lost in them. Maybe it happened because Brie was too much in her own head. Or maybe her mom was just *really* quiet that day. Whatever the reason was, Brie did not hear her mom's car pull into the driveway. She did not hear her open the front door.

She did not realize her mom was home until she was walking into Brie's bedroom. "Oh, good, you're home. I want to show you how to make the pasta sauce tonight."

Brie slammed her laptop shut and spun around, standing up quickly and nearly losing her balance. "Mom! Can't you knock?" Her voice was high and squeaky.

Her mom stared at her for a moment before glancing at the laptop—Brie moved her hand to hold it closed—and back at Brie. "What's going on?" she asked.

"Nothing," Brie said too quickly.

"What's on the laptop, then?"

"Nothing," Brie said again. "School stuff."

Her mom took another step into the room, and Brie suddenly felt as if there wasn't enough air in there for both of them. "What school stuff?"

"Mom, it's nothing. Stop."

Brie's face burned as she tried to keep her expression neutral, but her mom came closer and closer until they were practically nose to nose. Her mom reached for the laptop. Brie did not move her hand. "Let go, Brie."

"No. This is mine. It's private."

"The internet is not private—you know that," her mom said. "Let go."

Brie did not let go. Her mom grabbed the laptop anyway, yanking it out of Brie's grasp. This time, Brie *did* hear the front door open. "Dad's home. Please, Mom, just stop."

Her mom did not stop. She opened the laptop, where her Google Doc was still pulled up, front and center.

"Mom, *please.*"

"Is anyone home?" her dad called from downstairs.

Her mom sat down in Brie's computer chair. Scrolled through the document. Reached to hold her pendant tightly. Brie could do nothing but watch her.

Brie thought of all the scenes she had watched and added to her list. All the things that Brie was confused about were *right there* for her mom to see and be confused about, too.

Brie's vision blurred with tears as she realized it was all real now. That her mom had seen what she'd been Googling, that her mom knew what Brie had been thinking about. Brie could not come up with an excuse that would make it seem like something it wasn't.

And Brie didn't think she wanted to make excuses. Not anymore. She wasn't really ready . . . but *God*, she didn't want to lie anymore.

Her dad came up the stairs and stood outside Brie's still-open bedroom door. "What's going on in here?" he asked.

Brie turned to look at him, and now he knew *something*, too. Brie did not want him to know any more.

"Mom, just, *please*. That's *private*. We can—just let me . . ."

"Go downstairs, Gabrielle," her mom said.

"What?" She looked at her dad, who was standing there with a creased brow as he took in the scene. "Dad, she—"

"Phil, can you just . . ." Brie's mom was running her pendant back and forth on its chain. "I need her to . . ."

"Go on downstairs, Brie," her dad said. He reached out a hand to clasp her shoulder. Brie flinched at the contact. "We'll be down in a minute."

Brie did as she was told. What other choice did she have? She sat on the living room couch while her mom and dad were upstairs in her bedroom, going through her document and search history and God knows what else, talking about *her*, about *her* life and who *she* was, and Brie couldn't do anything except flip on the TV to her soap and try to focus on that instead.

But she couldn't. Everything about *General Hospital* just made her feel sick.

Her dad came downstairs nearly an hour later. "You and me are going to go get some food, kid."

Brie had a million questions. She didn't ask any.

Instead, she followed her dad into his car, and they sat in silence as they drove, the radio playing the classic rock her dad always listened to. Normally, Brie would change the station to something she liked, but she didn't do anything. She kept her eyes out the window as she leaned her head against the door, watching her neighborhood pass by as her dad drove them to Sissy's Diner.

Brie tried her best not to wonder why her mom wasn't with them, tried not to wonder what she was doing still at home.

They sat in a corner booth, and Brie liked the privacy. The waiter came over right as they sat down. "I'll have a coffee," her dad said.

"Me too," Brie added.

The waiter looked at her dad, who nodded with a soft laugh. "Guess you need one."

His laughter deflated something that had been growing inside her chest, and Brie exhaled deeply. "Is Mom mad?" she asked once the waiter left.

"Your mom is . . . confused," her dad said. Brie could tell he was choosing his words carefully. "I imagine you are, too."

Brie squirmed. "I don't . . . Do we have to talk about this?"

"We don't," her dad said. "And your mom . . . She didn't mean to violate your privacy. She was just concerned. She didn't realize what was going on."

"She could have asked," Brie said.

"Would you have told her?"

"No. But that's not the point." Brie looked around the diner. It was close to home, and everyone in their town came to it at some point or another. The booths were stacked along the walls, and the door continuously swung open as commuters going to and from the Belford Ferry stopped in for coffee. It was a little early for a big crowd, but there were still a lot of people. Brie wanted to make sure she didn't know any of them. "Is Mom . . . I mean, I don't . . ." She buried her face in her hands. "I don't know what I want to ask."

"Can I ask you a question?" he asked, his eyes on his menu.

Brie didn't really want him to. "What are you going to order?"

"I think a cheeseburger," he said, and then his eyes met hers. "Are you okay? Do you need us to find someone for you to talk to?"

Brie felt as though she might start crying. "Can I get chocolate chip pancakes?"

He watched her for a moment, not saying anything, and it struck Brie how thin his gray hair seemed, how many new wrinkles were on his face. He reached across the table to place his hand on top of hers. It was warm, and Brie was certain hers was still sweaty, but she didn't pull away. "Yeah, you can get the pancakes," he said. "I'll get you whatever you need."

11.

ALL MY CHILDREN, May 1993:
Kendall Hart reveals to Erica Kane that she's
Erica's daughter. If Bianca needs Erica to
see her, then Kendall needs Erica to want
her. Kendall feels a lot of pain, thinking that
she doesn't.

Brie's mom did not talk about what had happened. Neither
did Brie.

The week passed, and every moment Brie spent with her
mom, she felt a squeeze in her stomach, wanting to say something, wanting to bring it up, but not knowing how. Instead,
they talked about recipes as Brie's mom showed her how to
make different dinners. She made plenty of small talk—but
she never really said anything important.

Every minute of every day felt like the moment Brie got her period all over again. When she wanted to say *something* but just . . . couldn't. Didn't.

They also stopped watching soaps together. Brie knew it was her fault. Maybe her mom couldn't stomach them anymore, either, after reading Brie's document.

Brie didn't know if she wanted it to just . . . disappear, or if she wanted her mom to turn around in the middle of showing Brie how to roast potatoes, and say, "You know what? Let's talk about it." Because she didn't know which outcome she wanted more, Brie did nothing.

She also didn't use her laptop much. If she needed it for schoolwork, she kept her door open and did it quickly. It gave her pins and needles and butterflies. She wondered when those would go away.

It was easier to breathe at school, where she had Parker and Wallace and recess. But her dad was also there, fixing burned-out lights in the hall and working on sets during play practice. Kennedy was there, too, always seated front and center in class in the spot where Brie's eyes always ended up.

It seemed that no matter how hard she tried, Brie couldn't escape her feelings or the mess they'd put her in. Not really.

"Brie? Could you come here a moment?" Ms. Santos had them working quietly as she read through their latest homework assignments. They were starting to write essays based on prompts Ms. Santos gave them each week. This weekend Brie had stared at her blank piece of paper (she'd opted to write it longhand instead of typing it on her laptop), trying to pick an argument and defend her position on it.

When Brie walked up to Ms. Santos's desk—ignoring the fact that she could practically feel Parker's eyes on the back of her head—Ms. Santos offered her a smile. "I wanted to check in about your work."

Brie frowned. For the past month or so, she'd been turning in all her work on time and following all the directions. "Did I do something wrong?"

"Not at all," Ms. Santos said. There was a sudden commotion from the other side of the room, where Jack and Shaun were fooling around. "Boys, you should be doing your work," Ms. Santos scolded before focusing back on Brie. "Just, after our conversation last week, I've been doing some thinking, and I had an idea."

Brie started to feel a little claustrophobic, standing up by Ms. Santos's desk, surrounded by the rest of the desks and students in the room. "Oh?"

Ms. Santos glanced behind Brie, calling, "Kennedy? Could you come up here for a moment?"

Brie felt the pins and needles again. "Should I go back to my seat?"

"No, no, stay right here," Ms. Santos said.

Brie felt warm and a little wobbly as Kennedy made her way to Ms. Santos's desk. Brie averted her eyes. Kennedy hadn't asked to sit on the swings with Brie and her friends at recess or really talked to them much at all since Brie had been mean to her in class.

"Yes, Ms. Santos?" Kennedy said in that voice Brie used to call Kennedy's "suck-up voice." Just the thought of leaning over to whisper that to Parker made Brie's stomach hurt even more.

"I think the two of you have a lot more in common than you think," Ms. Santos said, and for a moment, Brie wondered if Ms. Santos really *had* seen through everything Brie had said the last time they'd talked. "I know the work in this class is getting to both of you lately, and I think it might be a good idea for you two to work together. Bounce some ideas off of each other, give feedback on each other's essays. What do you think?"

Brie glanced at Kennedy, who glanced back at her. Kennedy looked just as wary as Brie felt.

"Why?" Brie asked.

"We talked about how important peer review is, right?" Ms. Santos asked. They both nodded. "So why not give it a chance?"

Brie did not want to give it a chance.

But then Kennedy said, "Sounds good," and Brie felt obligated to agree.

When the bell rang, Kennedy hovered by the classroom door. Brie motioned for Parker to go ahead and save her a seat at lunch.

"So," Kennedy said.

"So," Brie replied.

"Do you want me to come over after school this week to work on our homework?"

Brie recoiled at the thought. The last thing she needed was Kennedy in her house, with her pretty hair and pretty smile, with Brie's mom there to see all of it, wondering if the way Brie looked at Kennedy meant nothing or if it meant that very *something* they weren't talking about. "I don't know my mom's work schedule, and she doesn't like when I have people over and she's not there," Brie said. "How about your house?"

Kennedy shifted her backpack to her other shoulder. A piece of hair fell out from behind her ear. It made Brie's nose burn. She felt so angry at that stupid strand of hair and how she really wanted to reach out and touch it. "Okay," Kennedy said, oblivious to her hair and Brie's feelings and how they were related. "I'll ask my parents what day works and get back to you."

Brie was relieved when Kennedy walked away. She didn't move, watching Kennedy make her way down the hall, until she saw her dad. He was fixing a light that was out in the hallway. He met her gaze, and Brie felt like he could read her mind because he knew too much, and she was angry all over again.

Three days later, Brie's dad drove her to Kennedy's house. She lived on the other side of the highway, in a big house with lots of windows. The front door was bright blue. There were two different doorbells and a knocker. Brie did not know which she was supposed to use, so she used all three.

Kennedy opened the door, flushed and out of breath. "Hi," she said. She was still wearing her school uniform, which put Brie a little at ease, since she was still in hers, too. School had let out nearly an hour ago, but she'd had to wait for her dad, and she hadn't gotten a chance to go home. "Come in. My mom's making us a snack, if you're hungry."

The inside of Kennedy's house was big. Brie craned her neck to look up at the chandelier that hung from the ceiling of the entryway. Brie had never seen a chandelier in real life before. Kennedy followed her gaze. "My dad designed the house," she said. "He said the one thing he knew he wanted was to make every room really bright."

He succeeded. Brie took in the light-colored walls and clean furniture as she followed Kennedy into the living room. Kennedy's little sister was kneeling on the floor in front of the coffee table, working on her homework, her backpack on the ground beside her and a pencil in her hand.

She looked up and smiled at Brie, the same wide smile as her sister, except with fewer teeth. "Hi!"

"That's my sister, Ella. My brother has hockey practice, so he's not around," Kennedy said. "Let me just go tell my mom you're here, and we can go up to my room."

Brie was surprised to find that unlike the spacious brightness of the rest of the house, Kennedy's room was cluttered and cozy. She had fleece blankets haphazardly thrown over the top of the purple comforter on her bed, and books in disordered piles along the gray walls. Her closet didn't have a door, and Brie could see that Kennedy's shirts were falling off their hangers and that the floor was buried beneath shoes and bags. Her walls were covered with posters, including some of Hillary Clinton and Rosie the Riveter. "You weren't kidding when you said you liked politics," Brie said, gesturing toward a retro-style *Votes for Women* poster.

Kennedy smiled. "I'm going to put myself in a position to make change someday. I hope, anyway."

"That's cool," Brie said. She hovered in the doorway before deciding to just sit on Kennedy's bed. It was warm, and the blankets were soft. "Oh, wow. I could fall asleep right here, right now."

Kennedy laughed. "I love blankets."

"I can tell."

Kennedy sat down next to her, and Kennedy plus the blankets made Brie feel even warmer. She picked at her fingernails, trying to figure out what to say next. "Ms. Santos said the work was getting to you, too?"

Kennedy shrugged. "She thinks I try too hard and stress myself out."

"Wow. I didn't know teachers could get on your case for trying *too* hard." Brie shrugged. "I've always gotten the 'you don't try hard *enough*' lectures."

"Yeah, I wanted to ask what changed," Kennedy said. "I mean, no offense, but I didn't think you really cared all that much about getting As and school stuff."

Brie's shoulders tensed. "That's because *no one* cares as much as you."

Kennedy flinched but didn't respond.

Brie felt like a jerk. She exhaled deeply. "Sorry," she mumbled. "I'm just . . ."

"Just what?"

"I'm trying to prove to my mom that I can be, you know . . . the daughter she wanted. So that I can audition for MCPA. Or at least, that's what started it. Now . . . I don't know." Brie picked at a run in her school tights. "I think she's mad at me. I'm trying to smooth things over."

Kennedy tucked her leg underneath the rest of her and reached over to pull one of the blankets over her lap and then over Brie's. "Why is she mad at you?"

Brie felt the familiar bubble start to form in her chest, the one that made her want to frown and say something mean so

Kennedy would back off. The bubble that blamed Kennedy for the things Brie was feeling, for the things Brie wished she didn't feel at all. This time, though, she swallowed it down. "She saw some things on my computer I didn't want her to."

Kennedy's eyes were wide. "My mom and dad don't ever look at our stuff. They say unless they have reason to believe we're in trouble, they wouldn't violate our privacy."

Brie scoffed. "Privacy does not exist on the internet, says my mom. But really?" She paused, sniffed back the sudden wetness in her nose. "I do kind of feel violated, I think. Or at least, I feel really weird about it all. It wasn't . . . I don't know. I didn't do anything bad. Or at least that's what my dad said. But I still feel weird about it."

"I'm sorry."

"You know how I told you I like soap operas?" Brie said, and Kennedy nodded. "Well, because they go on for so long and there's so many episodes and stuff, if an actor or actress doesn't want to be on the show anymore but the character is too important to just . . . kill off or whatever, they recast the role."

"Really?" Kennedy asked. "Like, a new actor just steps in? Isn't that weird?"

Brie shook her head. "It's not—that's the thing. They just . . . have them fill right in. A narrator voice will come on and say, 'The role of this character is now being played by . . . ,' and then the show just carries on as normal. I always really loved that."

Kennedy laughed. "I would, too. It sounds funny."

"It is," Brie said, smiling for a moment, thinking about how both she and her mom couldn't resist giggling every time it happened. "But also . . . I like that. I like that it gives this character a fresh start. It's the same character . . . but also new. I wish I could just do that, you know?"

Kennedy paused to think about it, leaning toward Brie. "Recast yourself?"

"Still be me, but new. Better, maybe." Brie's gut told her to move away, but instead she moved closer, wanting to feel Kennedy's warm breath on her face. She opened her mouth to say more, and at the same time, there was a knock at Kennedy's bedroom door right before her mom entered. Brie pulled away from Kennedy like a whip, her legs getting tangled in the blanket as she nearly fell off the bed.

"Oh! Didn't mean to startle you," Mrs. Bishop said. "I just wanted to bring you guys some cookies. Don't get too excited—they're just the slice-and-bake kind." She exaggeratedly winked, as if she were telling them a secret that was bigger than the one Brie had almost confided in Kennedy.

When her mom left the room, Kennedy looked at Brie, as if waiting for the conversation to pick right back up where they had left it. Brie reached for her backpack instead. "We should get our work done," she said.

Kennedy—Brie was grateful—followed her lead.

April

Six Sundays until
the May Crowning

12.

GENERAL HOSPITAL, March 2006:
Sam McCall finds out that Alexis Davis is actually
her birth mom. She wishes that it could have
been anyone else. They do not like each other,
and they have a long, long road ahead of them.

Brie sat in front of the TV with a Pop-Tart she was more crumbling up with her fingers than actually eating. *General Hospital* was on, but Brie wasn't watching it. Her mom wasn't home, but that didn't really matter. Whether she was at work or in the living room, the silence was the same.

When the door opened, Brie felt her entire body tense until she realized it was her dad. "Oh, good, you're home. Here," he said, reaching into his back pocket and pulling out his wallet. He took a card out from it and held it toward her.

Brie looked over at him, confused. "What is it?"

He gave her that sheepish smile of his, the one that was almost always on his face when he saw her in the school hallways. "What's it look like? My credit card. For that fancy arts-school application. You said you needed one, right?"

Brie froze. The buzzing inside of her made her want to jump and shout and squeal in the dramatic way her mom and her teachers sometimes scolded her for. But the truth of the matter was that Brie hadn't been thinking of MCPA much. Not since she'd been thinking mostly of . . . Kennedy. More specifically, of those feelings and her mom's reaction to them. Brie had seen the posters hung throughout town promoting the performance of *Much Ado about Nothing*, but she hadn't thought about the two tickets that sat on her desk in a while. The May Crowning was getting closer, too. But Brie's focus lately wasn't on any of those things—it was on getting her mom to talk to her again.

"Yeah, I do. I mean . . ." Brie said. "I . . . forgot."

Her dad placed the card on the coffee table in front of her, next to the Pop-Tart mess she had made. "Well," he said. "Here you go, then."

She felt like she might start crying. He started to walk away, probably to go fix himself a snack in the kitchen, but Brie called after him. "Dad?"

He stopped and turned around. "Yeah?"

"How're the sets for the play coming along?"

He smiled. A real one, which made him look younger, and which he hadn't had on his face in a while. Not that

Brie could remember, anyway. "Oh, uh, Diane Brophy just went over a bunch of things you guys'll need made. I'll probably get started next week. She wants them ready for you guys to have for, uh, what do you call it, the week of opening night."

"Tech week," Brie said. "That's when we practice for real, with costumes and lights and, well, the sets."

"Well, hopefully I get some good sets made before that, then." He gave her a little shy shrug and then turned to head into the kitchen.

Brie wasn't ready to let him go. "Hey, Dad?"

"Yeah?" he said eagerly, as if he had been waiting for her to extend a branch in the same way Brie was waiting on her mom to extend one to her.

Brie smiled at him. "I bet you'll do a really good job."

That night, now that her dad had put it back on her mind, Brie softly knocked on her mom's bedroom door. She had just arrived home from work and was getting ready for a shower. Brie's heart was beating fast. "Mom?"

"I'm about to get in the shower. What's up?" her mom said as she removed her jewelry, placing all the pieces on her dresser.

Brie was having trouble looking her mom in the eye, so she watched her go through her routine, keeping her gaze on her mom's earrings as she removed them, then letting her eyes drift down to watch as she took off her rings.

Her mom kept her Mary pendant on, and Brie couldn't look away from it.

Why is Mary so important to you, and is it okay that I don't feel that way? That all of this is so confusing? That my May Crowning essay will be terrible because I don't know, I just don't know *how I feel about all of it?*

"MCPA's play is next weekend," Brie said instead. "Are we still going? We've got the tickets."

Her mom sat down on the edge of her bed to pull off her socks. She didn't seem able to make eye contact with Brie, either. Brie stayed where she was, hovering over the threshold. "Oh no. Next weekend? I think I'm on the work schedule. I forgot. I'm sorry."

Brie wanted to argue. They'd gone to the play every year since Brie was in fourth grade. Just like they watched soaps together.

Apparently, neither was important to her mom anymore.

So Brie didn't argue. It was easier to pretend they were unimportant to her, too.

The following school week, the entire eighth grade gathered in the cafeteria during fourth period (which happened to be Mrs. Dwek's math class, so Brie was pleased). She, of course, sat next to Wallace, who—thanks to a fall during hockey practice—was sporting a pair of crutches that kept falling over onto her. It took a while for Brie to spot Parker, who was taller when she was standing than when she was sitting, but it didn't take long for Brie to find Kennedy four tables in front of her.

Wallace leaned over—crutches falling against Brie's shoulder again—to whisper loudly, "Being in here makes me hungry. It almost feels like a tease to my stomach."

"Okay, everyone, settle down," Mrs. Dwek addressed the students. A hush came across the cafeteria. Some unsettled whispers continued, but all eyes found their way up to the teachers who stood front and center in the room. "A reminder that just because we are in the cafeteria, that does not mean you can treat this like lunch or recess. Mind yourselves. Classroom rules apply."

Ms. Santos took over. "As you all know, the May Crowning is a little over a month away. We've been working for a few months now, learning essay structure and how to construct an impassioned speech. Sister Patricia has also spent a lot of time in your religion classes discussing the importance of Mary, Mother of God, and what she means to each of you."

"Oh *no*," Brie gasped. She should have seen this coming. But after these past few weeks dealing with her own mother, she felt completely blindsided.

"What's wrong?" Wallace asked.

"I'm not ready! They're going to make us write these *today*?"

"What I'm leading up to here is that you are all going to draft your May Crowning essays today," Ms. Santos confirmed.

"*No!*" Brie exclaimed—drawing out the *o*—to the entire cafeteria.

Ms. Santos raised an eyebrow. "Hopefully Brie doesn't speak for all of you. I promise you guys are ready for this. Now, Mrs. Dwek is going to hand out sheets of paper, but we'll have more if you need them. The prompt is simple: What does Mary, Mother of God, mean to you? We've talked a bit about interpretation, so remember, answer *your* interpretation of that question. You guys have until the end of the class period."

"No, no, no, no," Brie mumbled to herself as loose-leaf paper was passed around. She needed this. Needed it now more than ever, because it meant a lot to her mom—*Mary* meant a lot to her mom—and Brie needed to mean a lot to her mom again, too. She needed to prove that she was someone her mom could still like, that there were still bits of Brie that were worth talking to and spending time with and being proud of. She needed to do this so that maybe, just maybe, her mom could look at her with love in her eyes from the center of the church auditorium as Brie stood up on the altar in a pretty dress and crowned Mary. So that her mom could forget about the rest of it.

"This is so dumb," Wallace said. "I don't even *want* to crown Mary, and now I have to write this stupid essay all class."

Brie stared at the clean sheet of paper sitting in front of her. She wasn't ready for this. She needed to pull off a winning essay somehow. She had worked hard in Ms. Santos's class. In Sister Patricia's class, but did she even really stand a chance?

She still didn't have any answers.

It was too stuffy in the cafeteria, and Brie yanked off her sweater, even though she knew she'd get a dress code violation for the untucked blouse she had on underneath.

The room fell pretty quiet considering the number of eighth graders in it, as Ms. Santos, Mrs. Dwek, and Sister Patricia walked around to make sure everyone's eyes were on their own paper. Four tables away, Kennedy was already writing.

Wallace's crutches finally fell to the ground, and the echoing clash made everyone look toward the noise. Brie scowled at Wallace, who shrugged and left them on the floor. When she looked back up, she caught Kennedy's gaze. Kennedy gave her a small smile and a thumbs-up before turning back to work on her essay.

What did Mary, Mother of God, mean to Brie?

What did her *own* mother mean? What did *she* mean to *them*? God, what if Mary knew about Brie, about the things she Googled, about the things she felt, and what if she would look at Brie like Brie's mom did lately? What if she wouldn't like Brie, either? What if—

"Hey." A hand gently grasped her shoulder, and Brie jumped, looking up to meet Ms. Santos's eyes. She gave her what Brie assumed was supposed to be an encouraging smile. "Relax, Brie. I can practically hear you thinking across the cafeteria."

"I can't do this," Brie said. She wished she could unbutton her blouse. She was so sweaty.

Ms. Santos crouched down so that she could whisper. "Just write what you feel."

Brie's quiet laugh was wobbly. "What I feel is a hot mess."

"Then write about that," Ms. Santos said, as if it were the easiest thing in the world.

But . . . could she? Could she just write about Mary and her mom and her feelings and how everything was so messed up and confusing? Could she talk about how she had flutters in her stomach and flushed cheeks when she looked at Kennedy? That wasn't supposed to be okay, was it? Not here, anyway. Not in the center of a cafeteria with a crucifix on the wall, a nun patrolling the room, and a chapel down the hall.

But . . . but Bianca was brave enough to beg her mom to see her. And soaps were what Brie and her own mom had in common, right? That was their thing. It was *theirs*. And if Bianca could make Erica Kane see her, if Bianca could show her mom who she was . . . maybe Brie could do this, too. Maybe Brie could show her mom what she was feeling.

I want you to see who I am, Mother. Can you see who I am?

Brie took a deep breath, put her pen to her paper, and began.

※

By the time recess rolled around, Brie's brain was fried. She, Wallace, and Parker sat on their usual swings, but the other two must have been equally as fried, because no one really had much to say. Parker noted quietly that one of the clouds she had been staring at sort of looked like a giraffe, and Wallace said it looked more like the Eiffel Tower, and that was about the extent of their conversation.

Which is how Kennedy found them quietly staring up at the sky as she made her way over. "What are you guys doing?"

"Nothing," came the reply in chorus.

The bell rang, and the teacher on recess duty called them all to start lining up, so they got off their swings to slowly trudge their way back inside. "How do you think you did on the essay?" Kennedy asked, reaching for Brie's arm to pull her closer.

It was just as distracting as it always was, which made Brie flinch. "I don't really want to talk about it."

Kennedy nodded, looking down at her shoes as they continued walking. They got into linc, Parker in front of Brie in front of Kennedy, as Wallace got into the boys' line.

"Are you going to the hockey game Saturday? It's supposed to determine whether or not they make the play-offs," Kennedy said, then quickly shook her head. "Oh, no, you're probably going to the MCPA play, right? That's this weekend?"

Brie clenched her jaw. Kennedy was two for two in topics of conversation that made Brie's stomach hurt. "I was supposed to, but . . . not anymore."

"Oh," Kennedy said. The line began moving as they made their way inside. "Why not?"

My mom's avoiding me, Brie thought. "My mom has work," she said instead.

"I don't have to go to the hockey game. If you still want to go to the play," Kennedy said.

Brie knit her eyebrows together, confused.

Kennedy noticed. "With me, I mean," she added.

"Oh," Brie said. The heavy feeling that had been in her stomach since fourth period felt . . . different. She still felt like she might throw up, but she was able to breathe easier than she had all day. "I, uh. I have to ask if I still can. But yeah. Okay. If my dad says okay."

Kennedy exhaled into a smile. "Great. Text me later? I'll ask my mom, and then we can figure out what time to meet up and stuff."

As they got inside, Kennedy turned to go to her next class, and Parker stood staring at Brie, blocking the entrance to the science class they had together. "What?" Brie asked.

"You're hanging out with Kennedy a lot," Parker said.

The back of Brie's neck grew hot. "I mean, I guess. Not really, though."

Parker gave her a look.

"What?" Brie said, her voice a little higher than usual. "I told you Ms. Santos made us work together. That's not the same as hanging out."

Parker shrugged. "I thought you thought she was annoying."

"I did. I do." Brie pushed past Parker to go into science class. She looked up at the clock. Today really was just . . . not her day, and she needed it to be over. "It's not a big deal. It's not like she has any other friends. I'm just being nice."

Brie sat down heavily, dropping her backpack onto the ground loudly and resting her chin on the top of her desk. Parker took the seat next to her, even though that wasn't where she was supposed to be sitting. The late bell rang, but Parker didn't move. "I just . . ." Parker started, and then stopped.

"What?" Brie asked.

"We've just been hanging with Wallace a lot. And now you're spending time with Kennedy." Parker shrugged. "And I kind of feel like you don't really tell me things anymore."

Brie sat up. "That's not fair. You're the only one who knew my dad was working here. And I thought you liked hanging with Wallace."

"Brie, come on. You know what I'm saying." Parker's face was bright red. Brie was almost certain her own was pretty beet colored, too. "It's never just us anymore, and you've been really strange lately. What's going on?"

Brie didn't realize Parker was so perceptive. Or maybe she didn't realize she was being so obvious. Either way, she was really, *really* going to throw up. "Things are weird at home right now. That's all."

"Do you want to talk about it?" Parker asked.

She did. She really, really did. She wanted her mom to talk to her about it; she wanted to talk to Parker about it. Sometimes, she even wanted to open up and just tell Kennedy all about it. But the words were all tangled in Brie's head, like the mess of words she'd written in her essay about Mary that was supposed to fix everything. She just didn't know—she *never* knew—where to start or where to end or what would go in the middle. All she knew, really knew, was that she liked Kennedy—*liked* liked Kennedy—and that made things harder at home and harder at school and harder in her own head.

Parker disclosed her own crushes so easily and so often. Brie wanted so badly to be able to do the same. "I think I . . . like . . . someone," Brie said carefully.

Parker's face lit up. She practically bounced in her seat. "What? No *way*. Who?"

"Kennedy," Brie whispered. It shocked her how simply it came out.

"Oh," Parker said, forehead creased, until her eyes suddenly popped open wide. "Oh!"

With impeccable timing that Brie cursed under her breath, their science teacher, Mr. Strobel, made his way into the room right at that moment. He closed the door and told them to take out their homework assignments for him to check. Parker hesitated but then got up to go to her own seat across the room. Brie went back to resting her head on her desk.

Her phone, which she always kept hidden in her skirt pocket, vibrated against her thigh. She looked up to check that Mr. Strobel was still on the other side of the room, and quickly pulled it out to see she had a text from Parker. She opened it and had to blink back tears when she saw the rainbow and thumbs-up emoji Parker had sent.

Her eyes found Parker, who gave her a real thumbs-up to match the emoji.

Brie breathed easier than she had in months.

13.

GUIDING LIGHT, October 2002:

Reva Shayne gets herself arrested without fully thinking about the consequences. Her daughter, Marah, argues that everything is always about what Reva feels and what Reva is going through, when Marah needs Reva to stop and think about what Marah feels.

When Saturday came, Brie's dad drove her to Monmouth County Performing Arts. Every time she saw the high school, Brie was surprised that it didn't look much different from Red Bank Catholic, which was Trevor's high school, or even the public one Brie was supposed to be attending next fall. It was newer than the other schools but just as ordinary. She supposed the extraordinary came from what was inside.

She hoped so, at least.

"Call me when it's over," her dad said.

"I will." Brie took off her seat belt and started to open the car door.

"And hey, wait one sec," her dad said. "I just want you to know that your mom was sorry to have to miss this. I know you look forward to it every year."

Brie forced a smile. "It's fine."

She had a feeling they both knew it wasn't.

Kennedy was waiting for her at the front doors, and Brie handed her the extra ticket. "Do you know what this play is about?" Kennedy asked.

"Nah. It's supposed to be funny, though, I think."

"I didn't know Shakespeare was funny," Kennedy said.

"That's because they only ever make us read *Romeo and Juliet*." Brie was wearing a light-blue shirt that she'd borrowed from Parker. Parker had said it made Brie's eyes look nice. Parker was making it her mission to play matchmaker, so she'd texted Brie nonstop while she'd been getting ready. (Brie had realized pretty quickly that Parker didn't care *who* the crush was on. Parker loved every and all potential crushes equally.) Brie didn't know how the shirt made her eyes look nice—did brown and blue even match?—but the pins and needles felt a little less intense now that she had Parker on her side.

Brie had tried to tell Parker this wasn't a date. To Kennedy, it was probably just two friends hanging out at a high school play, because Kennedy felt bad that Brie had no one to go with.

Still, as they handed their tickets to the students that sat out in the foyer and Kennedy smiled at her, Brie couldn't help but feel butterflies.

It was only when they entered through the doors to the auditorium that Brie stopped thinking about Kennedy. She did this every time, took a moment to just . . . look. MCPA's auditorium was nothing like the one at OLPH. It was an actual theater, with cushioned seats and a real wooden stage and curtains and a balcony. There were no basketball hoops or scoreboards or bleachers. No church plants or altars.

It was real, in a way that OLPH's wasn't.

Brie, like she'd done every year since the fourth grade, pictured herself up on that stage, front and center, looking out at the audience instead of sitting in it.

"Wow," Kennedy said. "How cool."

"Let's find our seats," Brie said, glancing at the row and seat number on her ticket. They found their row easily. They were a little early, and Brie found herself staring at the thick red curtain that separated the actors from everyone else. Last year, the play had been *You're a Good Man, Charlie Brown*, and her mom had *loved* the girl who'd played Lucy. Her mom had thought the girl was hysterical and talented, and Brie wondered if that girl had been a senior last year or if she might be in this play, too. She wondered if one day—if next year—*she* could be the one on that stage whom her mom loved.

If her mom would even come to see her at all.

I want you to see who I am, Mother.

"Are you okay?" Kennedy's voice startled Brie.

"What? Oh, I'm fine," Brie said. "Just . . . waiting for the show to start."

Kennedy kept her eyes on Brie, and Brie felt a little too warm as more and more people took their seats around them.

"You just seem—I don't know. Kind of . . . off," Kennedy said.

Brie exhaled. "I'm supposed to be here with my mom," she said and then cringed. "Sorry. I mean, I'm happy I'm here with you. I just . . ."

Kennedy reached over and took Brie's hand. Brie nearly forgot how to breathe. She hoped Kennedy didn't notice. "It's okay," Kennedy said. "I understand."

Brie was glad the lights suddenly went down. She was even more glad that the curtain went up, the play began, and Kennedy did not let go of her hand.

She couldn't stop thinking about how sweaty her palm must be or how soft Kennedy's hand was or how Parker would be freaking out about this if she were here to see it. It was distracting in the best way, in the most confusing way, in a way that made Brie's stomach feel funny, and she had to keep reminding herself to focus on the stage.

And when she did pay attention to the show, she liked it. She liked getting lost in the story as much as she got lost in the feel of Kennedy's hand. She liked watching two people who bickered and didn't like each other fall in love.

After all the hurt and confusion and lies, happily ever after happened anyway.

＊

Parker came over the next day, because she *couldn't wait* to talk about Brie's date.

"But it wasn't a date," Brie said for the third time as she and Parker sat in Brie's bedroom. It was a rainy day; the wind and raindrops beat loudly against Brie's window.

"Oh, potato tomato." Parker waved her off as she flipped mindlessly through a book she'd pulled off Brie's bookcase. "If it looks like a date and quacks like a date."

Brie laughed. "You just combined like four different sayings and got them all wrong."

"My point still stands," Parker said. "Anyway, did you like the play? Oh! Were there any cute boys?"

Brie rolled her eyes.

"You know," Parker continued, "I'm kind of glad you and I won't ever like the same person. Gives me more freedom."

"What do you mean?" Brie asked.

"Well, you know . . ." Parker shrugged. "I'm not going to have crushes on girls. Are you going to have crushes on boys?"

"I don't know," Brie said honestly. "I mean, maybe not. But also I could, maybe? It's all still a little confusing. I think I just like girls. But I'm only thirteen. It's not like I know a big pool of boys outside of OLPH."

"It's a pretty beautiful pool, if you ask me, but I get it. Maybe you do, or maybe you don't. You're still figuring that out." Parker nodded.

"Yeah," Brie agreed. "I guess I am."

There was a sharp knock at the door, and Brie sucked in her breath. Her mom opened it and stuck her head in. "Brie, this door stays open when you have friends over," she said. "Hello, Parker."

"Hi, Mrs. Hutchens," Parker said.

This was a new rule. "Since when?" Brie asked. "We're just talking."

Her mom sighed. "Don't argue with me."

"But that's stupid. Why do we need to keep the door open?" Brie asked, raising her voice. She could see how pink Parker's face was getting. Parker hated confrontation.

Her mom's hand gripped the doorknob tightly. "You know why, Brie. We can talk about this more later."

Her mom didn't give her a chance to argue, unless Brie wanted to shout her objections as her mom made her way back down the hall.

"What was that about?" Parker asked.

"Nothing," Brie said. "My mom's just in a mood."

It didn't feel like nothing, though. Brie felt like crying. Her conversation with Parker suddenly felt too personal to continue with the door open.

Brie didn't like it. She knew that everything that was happening was confusing and weird, but—until now—Brie hadn't felt as though she was any different. Her mom clearly did not agree.

"Well," Parker said. "Can we talk more about Javi? Wallace said he scored two goals yesterday! I think he may be the one."

Great, Brie thought as Parker continued talking about Javi. At least one of them was comfortable discussing her crushes with the door wide open and the entire house able to overhear.

14.

AS THE WORLD TURNS, June 1990:
Margo Hughes's stepdad begs her to make a
medical decision for him, even though her mom
will never forgive her for it. Still, she does what
she thinks is right, what she thinks she has to,
even if it drives a wedge between them.

It was Easter. Which meant that Brie was in an uncomfortable dress in an uncomfortable church pew next to her older
brother, who always seemed to forget to wear deodorant on
the days Brie was forced to be in close proximity to him.

His allergies also made him sniff up snot every five seconds. "Stop—you're so annoying!" Brie whispered as loudly
as she could without her parents overhearing.

Trevor flipped her off without them seeing. Brie was
pretty certain that was some kind of sin.

She'd been thinking about sins a lot lately. Since her mom had taken on extra shifts at her retail job and her dad went to church only when her mom made him (which basically meant holidays), Brie hadn't been to mass outside of school in a while. That suited her just fine. With her new . . . *awareness* . . . of certain things about herself, and knowing the church's stance on it, Brie spent the majority of mass praying that the priest wouldn't say anything negative about her feelings in his homily.

Her mom was sitting there listening intently, gaze never wavering from the priest and fingers toying with her pendant. If the homily said something—anything—about sexuality or Sodom or Leviticus or any of the words and stories in the Bible that got twisted up like Brie's stomach . . . her mom would hear it. And if she heard it . . . would she look at Brie? Would her dad?

She was so tense her shoulders would probably hurt all through their Easter meal. She supposed that was why she was taking her frustrations out on Trevor, but also, he really did smell. "You stink, Trevor," Brie said. "Can you at least move over?"

"Brie, shut up," he replied.

"Knock it off, you two," her mom chimed in.

Brie growled under her breath. Trevor heard her anyway. "Just daydream or something," he said.

"What?" she asked.

Trevor motioned with his chin to the priest at the altar. "If this is bothering you, just daydream. That's what I do."

Brie was confused for a moment, wondering why on earth Trevor would say that, until the penny dropped and she realized. "You *know*?"

He sighed. "The house is small, Brie. It's not a big deal."

"It is a big deal!"

"Shh!" her mom scolded. "I said knock it off."

Brie's mood didn't improve throughout mass or after mass or as her mom made her help prepare the ham they were cooking for dinner. Her mom's sisters were coming with their families, as well as Brie's grandparents, and Brie was already exhausted thinking about it. She usually loved Easter. Not really for religious reasons (she'd never tell her mom that), but because her grandma always made the *best* ricotta pie, and her aunt always made stuffed artichokes, and her mom always picked up the biggest and sweetest loaf of Easter bread she could find.

But instead, Brie was still reeling from finding out that Trevor knew. She really didn't want her grandparents or aunts or anyone else to know. Would they notice that her mom never really looked at her anymore? Would they ask Brie about boys in front of her? (God, what would her mom do if they did?)

Would they talk about the May Crowning, which Brie had lied about months ago, or about Brie's future or about all the things that Brie wasn't sure if she could talk about in front of them, in front of Trevor, in front of her mom and dad?

"I don't feel well," she said as she helped her mom put the ham in the oven.

"The family will be here soon," her mom responded.

Brie's nose started to burn. "I have cramps. Can I just go lie down?"

Her mom closed the oven and stood, looking at Brie with a question on her face. She wasn't due for her period for another two weeks, and her mom—who did the shopping—knew that better than Brie did. Especially since Brie had forgotten to mention the timing last month, causing a fight with her mom when she had to go out last minute to buy supplies.

But still, to Brie's surprise, her mom said, "Go lie down. I'll come get you for dinner."

She didn't really know why she was crying, just that her pillow was now damp as she listened to the commotion from downstairs. She could smell dinner from her bedroom, and her stomach growled, but she wasn't ready to face anyone yet.

There was a soft knock on the door, but her mom didn't immediately barge in like normal. "Come in," Brie mumbled into her pillow before reaching up to wipe her face.

Her mom walked in. "You okay?" she asked.

Brie tried really hard not to start crying again. "Just don't feel good."

"*Well*, you don't feel *well*, and what's wrong?" she asked, coming to sit at the foot of Brie's bed. "You sure it's cramps?"

"I don't know. I just don't feel *well*."

"Dinner's ready. And everyone is asking about you," her mom said. "Think you can handle coming down for the meal?"

Brie shrugged. Her mom placed a hand on Brie's leg, rubbing up and down her thigh. Brie closed her eyes, wet with tears, as she tried to enjoy spending time with her mom. She couldn't remember the last time they'd sat alone in a room without it being weird.

It still was weird. But it was kind of nice, too. "I'm sorry, Mom," Brie said. She wasn't even sure what she was apologizing for, just that she really, really wanted to say it.

Her mom didn't say anything, and when Brie turned to look at her, she realized her mom's eyes were shining, too. She was staring at one of Brie's walls, looking at nothing, or maybe looking at the fake Emmy Award on her dresser, the stacks of soap opera magazines on her desk. She waited for her mom to reach for the pendant around her neck, but she didn't. Her chest rose and fell with each breath she took, and Brie tried to match it, a breath for a breath, but her mom was breathing too fast for Brie to keep up. "Do you want me to bring you up a plate, then?" her mom finally asked.

Brie knew if she opened her mouth, she would start crying, and she really, really was trying not to do that. She nodded, chewing on the inside of her cheek, even though what she wanted was to ask her mom to stay, to not go anywhere, to just keep rubbing her leg instead of her pendant.

But she patted Brie's leg and stood up. "I'll go get that ready, then."

Her mom crossed the room, and Brie buried her face back in her pillow. "Mom?" she said, keeping her face hidden. "Thank you."

Brie expected to hear her door open and close or her mom to say you're welcome, and when neither happened, she picked her head up to look toward the door. Her mom was standing there, looking back at her, an odd expression on her face. "I love you, Brie," she said.

Brie hadn't realized until that moment how much she'd needed to know that. "Love you, too."

Brie did not feel refreshed after Easter break. It was a week off from school spent walking on eggshells around her mom and worrying every time Parker came over that she would say something about Kennedy that someone would overhear as they sat in her bedroom with the door open.

It was a relief, really, when school started again.

"Homework, Brie?" Ms. Santos was walking up and down the aisles in the classroom, checking the homework assignment that Brie had completely forgotten was due.

She stared down at her worksheet, as if she was shocked that it was unfinished. "Oh," she said. "I didn't . . . I forgot."

Ms. Santos hovered for a moment, frowning, and Brie flushed under the weight of it. She marked it down in her gradebook and turned to Wallace. His worksheet was complete.

"Wait, Ms. Santos—I have a question," Brie said, getting her attention back. "Do you know when they're going to announce who gets to crown Mary?"

Her question caused a couple of other students' ears to perk up. "The end of the month, probably. The readers are still, well, reading."

The eighth-grade faculty and a few others were supposed to read all the essays without knowing whose was whose. The best essay would be chosen for being the best, not because of a particular student. Brie hoped to God that was true. Because if her essay was terrible and she wasn't chosen . . . please, *please* let no one recognize her.

She might have written a little *too* honestly about her relationship with her mom.

Ms. Santos started up the aisle again to check more assignments.

"Ms. Santos?" Brie called again.

Ms. Santos gave her a smirk. "Let me check everyone else's homework, okay, Brie?" Three rows over, Shaun was frantically filling out his worksheet in the spare time Brie was giving him.

"Just one more question. Promise," Brie said. "I wanted to know if *you* read the essays yet."

"I did," Ms. Santos said, and Brie bit the inside of her cheek. "Now how about you start filling in those answers while I finish up here, okay?"

"Did you . . . I mean, were you able to, like, figure out whose essay was whose?"

Ms. Santos glanced over at Shaun, clearly onto him. She smiled gently at Brie. "Even if I was able to, you know I can't tell you anything," she said, then motioned to Brie's worksheet, blank on her desk. "Get to work, and let me finish up here."

Brie slumped back in her seat as Ms. Santos continued checking papers. Wallace slid his sheet over for Brie to copy his work, so at least she'd have the answers to study later, but Brie didn't feel much like bothering.

After forty impossibly long minutes, the bell rang, and everyone slowly gathered their things to go to their next impossibly long class. Parker was waiting for Brie at the door, and Brie fought with the zipper on her backpack to get it shut so she could catch up with her.

"Hey, Brie?" Ms. Santos called as Brie walked past her desk.

"Yeah?"

Ms. Santos leaned across the desk, as if she were going to confide all her secrets in Brie. Brie blushed as she leaned close, too. "Between you and me, I'd like to think that yes, I can tell my students' writing from one another, especially this far into the school year."

Brie felt heat spread up the back of her neck. "Oh."

"You look a little terrified."

Brie attempted a laugh, but it was definitely just a whimper. "I think I am."

"It's brave, you know?" Ms. Santos said. "Writing an honest essay, really putting your heart into it, it's very brave."

"I didn't know what to write."

"You wrote your truth," Ms. Santos said. "And I don't know what the results will be. I can't even really make a guess. But that essay I read? It was beautiful, Brie. Don't be embarrassed. Be proud, because there was a lot in that essay to be proud of."

Brie swallowed. "Really?"

Ms. Santos nodded her head in a way that seemed so confident and sure, Brie wanted to believe it. "Yes. I don't know what the outcome of anything is going to be, but that I'm sure of."

"Thanks, Ms. Santos."

"You are very welcome," Ms. Santos said. "But next time, do your homework."

15.

ONE LIFE TO LIVE, May 2008:
Adriana Cramer refuses to speak to her mother,
Dorian, after Dorian tries to sabotage Adriana's
relationship. Dorian tells her she'll understand
one day, when she has kids, that a mother does
whatever she has to for her children.

Tech week was only a couple of weeks away. Parker was currently being fitted for her costume as the old hag, who tricked Snow White into eating the apple. Brie was a big fan of the long, crooked nose with the big pimple on top that Parker had to wear. Parker was not as excited about it.

The forest animals and all seven dwarfs got to pick their costumes out of a big bin. A million eager hands pushed their way into that bin to pull out the most-desirable hats and shoes and shirts. Brie let everyone else go first. She didn't really care what she wore. She was still, well, *grumpy* over the casting. Especially when Parker looked so awesome and Deena, as Snow White, looked really pretty.

She cared a little more, of course, when she realized she was stuck with a bright-purple hat and Big Bird–yellow slacks and a striped shirt that was definitely too big. But at least she didn't end up dressed like a little white forest bunny with a big fluffy tail like Jack did.

"Okay, everybody, settle down. Come form a circle so we can get started," Ms. Brophy said as everyone pulled at Jack's floppy ears and laughed at the rip Shaun got in his Dopey pants.

"We'll fix that, Shaun—settle in. Now, I want to run lines with Snow White and the Evil Queen in their costumes, but I'm going to have Nico take the rest of you and work out your blocking during those scenes. So Parker, Deena, come with me. The rest of you get to work up on the stage," Ms. Brophy said.

That suited Brie fine, even if she had to be separated from Parker. Brie liked working with Nico. Nico's hair was black and purple and always pulled back in two high ponytails that stuck out as if they'd been electrified. She wore a lot of dark eye makeup, which she always applied in the bathroom after school, since she wasn't allowed to wear it during the day at the high school. "All right, let me have Sleepy and Dopey over here," Nico said, gesturing to Brie and Shaun.

"I'm Grumpy," Brie corrected.

"Close enough," Nico replied. "Come over here. You'll be sitting back here, right, but stay in character even if the focus is on Snow White. So, you know, do the grumpy and dopey thing while you hang back here."

"How should I do the dopey thing?" Shaun asked.

"Just be yourself," Jack said, causing Shaun to shove him.

Nico rolled her eyes. Brie figured Nico would have to *love* theater to want to put up with Brie's class. Either that or Ms. Brophy had bribed her.

"Nico, can I ask you a question?" Brie said as she got into her place.

Nico shrugged one shoulder as she moved Anthony—who was Doc—into position.

"If you like acting so much, why didn't you go to MCPA?"

Nico scrunched up her nose. "You two, woodland-creature dudes, over there." She pointed toward the other side of the stage and then focused back on Brie. "I didn't get in," she said.

Brie gasped. "But you're so good!"

Anthony agreed. "Ms. Brophy says you were her favorite."

"Yeah, well, I was a big fish in a small pond, and an average fish in a bigger one."

Brie didn't like the sound of that.

She was about to say so and to ask questions like *Are you sure you picked a good monologue?* and *Were you maybe having a bad audition day?* and *Do you think anyone else at this school stands a chance if you didn't even get in?* But before she could, something caught Nico's eye, and her usually expressionless face (unless she was performing) was suddenly full of expression.

"Whoa," Nico said, and everyone followed her gaze.

Brie's jaw dropped. If she was shocked by Nico's rejection, she was absolutely stunned by this.

Her dad was there, at the back of the auditorium, with large panels that were put together to look exactly like a forest. Tall trees lined the background, and leaves dangled along the top. The wood looked real—was it real? Had her *dad* done that? There were colorful birds perched in the trees, and the parts of the sky that were visible between the brush were orange and red and pink and yellow, like the sun was setting.

It was beautiful. It was perfect.

Brie jumped off the stage without waiting for permission and jogged to the back to meet her dad. The other students, along with Nico and Ms. Brophy, followed. "Dad! That's awesome! Did you make this?"

He scratched the top of his head, which was dusty. He must have just finished working on it, as indicated by the paint smears on his shirt, which were definitely going to make her mom angry. "I had some of Ms. Brophy's art-club students help with the paint, but I, uh, yeah. I put this together for you."

"Mr. Hutchens! It's wonderful," Ms. Brophy said. "Everyone, thank Mr. Hutchens for his hard work!"

The class thanked him, moving to look all around the backdrop, admiring his work. He smiled, looking more proud of himself than Brie thought he'd looked since he'd lost his job. It made her even more proud of him, too. She wrapped an arm around him, not caring if her classmates saw, as he kissed the top of her head.

That afternoon, Brie told her mom all about her dad's work during commercials as they sat in the living room, *not* watching *General Hospital* (even though it was 3:37, and *General Hospital* was on from 3:00 to 4:00). They were watching *Law & Order* reruns instead. "You'll come to the play, right? I don't really have many lines, but at least you can admire Dad's sets while I act all grumpy," she said.

"When is it again?" Brie's mom asked. "I don't think we ever put it on the calendar. You didn't seem so keen on us attending when you first got your role."

"It's two Fridays from now. And I changed my mind. I want you and Dad to come," Brie said. "Trevor, too."

148

Her mom frowned as she pulled out her cell phone to check her calendar on it. When her mom's shoulders fell, Brie slumped in her seat, too. "I'm scheduled to work that weekend."

"You can't come?" Brie asked. "But I only went out for this stupid play so that you could see that I can do this!"

"You were just talking as if you *liked* the play, and *now* it's stupid?"

"It's stupid if you don't come! Take off. Call in sick."

Her mom pinched the bridge of her nose, leaning over to rest her elbows on her knees. "It's not like I . . . You know I'd come if I could, but we need this job, Brie. If I can't get off . . . it's because I need to be *there*."

"You needed to be there instead of the MCPA play with me, too," Brie said, standing up. "Whatever. I don't care. And this TV show sucks. It's the same thing every episode."

"Brie, don't be like that."

"Be like what? I said I don't care," Brie said. "I'm going to my room."

"Hey, wait a minute," her mom said. "Come on, come sit back down. We were having a nice afternoon—"

"And you ruined it!" shouted Brie. "*You* did, not me. You haven't watched soaps with me in months and you barely talk to me and you work all the time and you don't know me at all, Mom, even though you think you do because you're nosy, but you don't!"

"What's all the shouting about?" Brie's dad asked as he entered the room.

All three of them fell quiet. Brie shifted her weight from one foot to the other, looking down at the tear in her tights. "Dad worked really hard on those sets," she mumbled.

Her mom looked at her dad, who blushed, and then back at Brie. "I don't work this job because I don't want to be here. Don't put that on me, Brie. I'm working incredibly hard for this family."

Brie's dad was looking down at his feet. Brie felt bad. Her mom had to work because he'd lost his job. Neither of them was at fault, not really, and in that moment her dad didn't look like he knew that. "I'm sorry," Brie said, and she meant it. "But I'm working hard, too. Because you told me to, with this play, and . . ." She paused for a moment but decided not to mention the May Crowning. "And I'm working hard in class, because you said I had to pull my weight, and I am. I'm pulling."

"I know you are. I see that. And I promise you I'm going to try and get off work. I'll really try, okay?" her mom said. Brie found herself nodding. "Now come on. Come sit back down, and watch the rest of this with me."

Brie glanced at her dad, who stood silently watching the two of them, his worry wrinkles deep, as he waited to see if their fight would keep going. Her mom sat back down on the couch, patting the seat next to her, *Law & Order* still playing in the background.

It wasn't the same. Still, Brie took a seat. "Okay."

She sank into the couch, closer to her mom than she'd originally been sitting, and when her mom wrapped an arm around her, Brie rested her head on her shoulder. "You'll really, really try?" Brie asked.

"Yes," her mom said, pressing a kiss to the top of Brie's head. "I'll really, really try."

16.

DAYS OF OUR LIVES, September 1993:
Sami Brady finds out about her mom's affair,
and begs her mom not to tell her dad about it.
Marlena promises she won't.

DAYS OF OUR LIVES, January 1994:
Marlena breaks her promise.

Her mom didn't get off work for the play. She couldn't. So there Brie was, arms folded across her costumed chest, her face set in an expression that would be perfect for the play, if only she were acting.

Her dad and Trevor would be there, at least. Trevor promised Brie's dad he would help move the sets. "Your mom did try, Brie. Don't think she didn't," her dad said as they pulled into the school parking lot.

"I know," Brie said, because she was supposed to. This conversation was starting to become part of their routine.

"It's . . . She has to work. And that's not on her, okay?" he continued. "If anything, that's on me."

"Dad, I really don't want to talk about it," Brie said.

It was always weird to be at the school at night, weirder still for it to be full, in that chaotic way that always happened as parents dropped their kids off, dressed up like little woodland animals and dwarfs and hunters and hags. Ms. Brophy and Ms. Santos did their best to usher the student actors behind the stage. Brie sulked alone as Grumpy.

"Hey," Ms. Santos greeted, pulling at the point on Brie's dwarf hat so it stood up straighter. "Break a leg, Brie."

Brie felt heat rise up the back of her neck. "Thanks," she mumbled.

Truth be told, Brie was still bummed, and maybe a little bit jealous of Parker and Deena and everyone else who would get to shine tonight. She had hardly any lines, just some cranky comments, and she mostly stood around in the background.

When it was finally showtime, Nico and Ms. Santos started telling them all to *"hush!"* and the murmurs in the audience grew quiet as the floor lights went down and they were all covered in darkness. Brie was surprised she had jitters and butterflies. Parker, before taking her spot, squeezed Brie's hand. Both of theirs were sweaty.

Then the stage lights lit up, with Deena—Snow White—front and center. Brie, from the side of the stage, behind the curtain, looked out at the audience and couldn't see any faces, couldn't tell who was Wallace or Mrs. Dwek or anyone. It was strange. It seemed very much as if no one were out there, when she knew everyone was. She imagined being front and center someday, completely alone onstage in a crowded theater, delivering a monologue clear and loud and emotionally. She imagined her mom and dad in the audience (and not at work or backstage moving sets), smiling up at her. She imagined doing well and getting applause and going on to star in soaps on TV and watching her scenes with her mom.

She imagined everything *tonight* wouldn't be.

Parker, though, was great. Brie could hear the slight tremor in her voice as Parker said all her lines, but she delivered them clearly and was delightfully evil. Brie even had to admit that Deena made a wonderful Snow White. She was soft and gentle in ways Brie wasn't even sure she could act, let alone be, and the audience applauded loudly after her first scene.

When it was Brie's turn, when the dwarfs walked out, the audience, which she still couldn't see, suddenly erupted in laughter. Something in that moment—laughter in front of her and her father's beautiful backdrop behind her—changed everything, and Brie had to remind herself not to smile. She said her first line, and more people laughed, and suddenly she wasn't grumpy. She was *acting* as Grumpy, and her heart thumped hard in her chest. She felt lighter and excited, saying each of her few lines, hoping for more laughter, for more applause.

She got both, and she loved it.

So, okay, no, it wasn't what Brie had imagined. She wasn't Snow White; she wasn't the star. But when the lights came up and they all took one another's hands to bow, Brie smiled wide. It was her first ever play in a career where she hoped there would be many. She would remember this forever.

Admittedly, though, she was happy to get out of her costume when it was all said and done. "I can't get the glue off my nose!" Parker said as the girls all changed in the dressing room. Parker was happy to get out of hers, too.

"Here, let me see," Brie said, reaching to pick off the glue left by Parker's fake long, crooked nose. "Tilt your head so I can get this piece."

The moment Parker tilted, she was no longer blocking Brie's view of the door, and Brie saw Kennedy standing there. Kennedy's hair was the way Brie liked it, with that strand falling loose and into her face, and she stood awkwardly in the doorway, lifting her hand in a small wave. Brie forgot what she was even doing.

"Did you get it?" Parker asked.

"Oh, sorry," Brie said and removed the last glue chunk from Parker's nose. "You're good now."

"You want to go out and find our parents?" Parker asked.

"I'll meet you out there," Brie said.

Parker turned to see where Brie was looking. Her face lit up. "Ah, yes. Go talk to your girl first."

Brie playfully shoved her. Then she walked over to greet Kennedy. "Hi."

"Hi," Kennedy replied.

"I didn't know you were coming."

"Of course I came. I knew you and Parker were in it," she said. "I sat with Wallace. You guys were so good."

Brie blushed. "I didn't do much. Parker was great, though."

Kennedy smiled, rocking back and forth on her heels. "You were so funny! I couldn't stop laughing. You totally belong onstage."

Brie's cheeks felt hot. She looked down at her toes. The dressing room was empty; everyone else had already changed and headed into the audience to find their families. It looked like a tornado had hit the room, costumes half-hung on hangers and makeup tubes all over the counters. "We should go out so I can find my dad," Brie said.

"Oh! Right, okay," Kennedy said. She was still balancing on her heels, and it was making that strand of hair drift back and forth across her face.

Brie couldn't take it anymore. She reached out to brush it behind Kennedy's ear. Kennedy stilled, and so did Brie, her fingers touching the skin of Kennedy's earlobe, which was softer than Brie had thought earlobes could even be. "Sorry," she whispered, realizing how close they were. Could Kennedy feel Brie's breath against her face? Did she like it?

Brie got her answer the moment Kennedy suddenly leaned forward and kissed her.

Brie was too stunned to do anything.

Kennedy pulled back and cringed, and Brie felt as though her face were on fire. "Um," Kennedy said, taking a step back. "I, uh . . ."

And then Brie realized what was happening. She was in an empty dressing room, costumes scattered about, as she stood in her yellow tights and ratty gray hoodie, sweaty from being onstage and from being here with Kennedy, and Kennedy had *kissed* her. *Kennedy* had kissed *her.* "Oh my God."

"I'm sorry. I just—"

Brie leaned forward and kissed her back.

✳

"Oh my *gosh*! Tell me *everything*!"

Brie had to hold her cell phone away from her ear. She was certain Parker's shrieks would shatter an eardrum if she wasn't careful.

Brie glanced at her bedroom door. Of course, she couldn't actually tell Parker everything—knowing her parents could, and would, pop in whenever they very well felt like it—but it still felt safer than texting it out for her mom to possibly find and read later. Brie gathered her thoughts to try to have this conversation without actually saying any of the details.

Kennedy wasn't her first kiss. She wasn't even her second. Shaun Frankel was her first kiss, back in sixth grade. A bunch of them had met at the movie theater on a Friday night. Brie had turned to ask him for some M&M's, and he'd kissed her. When her mom had picked her up, her face had still been pretty pink. Her mom had given her a knowing smile, and Brie had told her what had happened.

Her mom had made *such* a *big deal* about it. (*Your first kiss! Do you like him? Is he cute? Are you going to go on another movie date?*) So Brie did not tell her when Javi kissed her at the seventh-grade school dance the following year.

She sure as heck wasn't going to tell her about this one, either.

Brie lowered her voice as much as she could without sounding suspicious. "It happened quick. After you left the dressing room."

"You kissed her?"

"No," Brie said with a disbelieving shake of her head. She flopped back onto her bed and stared at the ceiling. "The other way around."

"No *way!*" Parker squealed, and then sighed. "I wish someone would spontaneously kiss *me*." She might have been boy crazy, but she had not yet been kissed. "I didn't even know Kennedy was, you know. Whatever."

Brie assumed *whatever* meant *queer.* "Me either. I mean, maybe she's not? I don't know. But she . . . did what she did . . . and then I did it back . . . and I think that means she . . . you know . . ." It was hard talking in half sentences.

"She obviously likes you," Parker confirmed. "She wouldn't have kissed you otherwise."

Brie considered that. The entire moment was so fuzzy in her head. She'd been sweaty from being onstage and from the nerves of being alone with Kennedy, and she'd been shocked by Kennedy's kiss and then had to leave to meet her dad and brother. "Should I text her?" Brie asked.

Parker said, "Hmm. Maybe tomorrow? Aren't you supposed to, like, wait a bit or something?"

"How would I know?" Brie said. "Everything is so . . . confusing."

"She kissed you, she likes you. How's that confusing?"

Brie didn't know how to explain.

There was a knock on her door, and she turned to see her dad standing in her doorway. "Park, I gotta go. I'll talk to you later." Parker said goodbye, and Brie ended the call. She sat up in the bed. "Hi, Dad. Is Mom home yet?" she asked.

"Should be home soon," he said as he fiddled with her doorknob.

Actually, she noticed he was leaning against the door, letting it support most of his weight as he slouched into it.

He wiped a hand over his face. "I just wanted to say you did good tonight," he said.

"Thanks," Brie said. "You did good, too. I mean, with the sets."

He smiled. It was a sleepy smile, but Brie loved it anyway. He nodded and turned to leave, and suddenly Brie really, really didn't want him to. She couldn't tell her mom. Her mom was barely talking to her. But her dad . . .

"Hey, Dad?" Brie called before he could turn away. She had the same feeling she'd had the first time she'd put on her costume—before she'd gotten used to the heaviness of the extra layers of clothes, before she'd gotten used to the suffocating cling of her yellow tights. She'd felt as though she would be uncomfortable no matter what she did, no matter how much she adjusted things. That was how she felt now, even in her most comfortable pajamas.

She took a deep breath. "I kissed Kennedy tonight. I mean, she kissed me. I mean, we kissed. Me and Kennedy."

"Oh," he said.

Oh no. That . . . couldn't be right. That couldn't be all. "Oh?" Brie repeated.

The discomfort grew worse when he wiped a hand over his face again and said, "That's . . . okay. Good, right? I mean, yeah, I really need to get some sleep, Brie. I'm not feeling great. I'll see you in the morning, okay?"

It was something she would expect from her mom but not from him, and it *hurt*. "Oh, okay," she said. "I'll see you tomorrow."

"You were really great tonight."

"Thanks," she said, and he turned and left her.

When her mom came home, Brie was still awake, anxiety buzzing up from her stomach to her throat as she stared at her ceiling. Her bedroom light was still on, so it was no surprise when her mom came to knock on the frame of the cracked-open door. "You're still awake?"

"Still too wired," Brie said. It wasn't a total lie.

"How'd it go?"

Brie half-heartedly shrugged. "It was fine."

"You're mad at me for not being there."

"It's fine. I'm just tired."

"I'm proud of you, Brie," her mom said, and Brie wanted her to leave. She should have just pretended she was already sleeping. "I'm going to make your dad tell me all about it tomorrow."

Brie was certain her stomach would never stop hurting again.

So much for first performances. So much for first-crush kisses.

It was a long weekend of barely there conversations with her parents, and being home was starting to hurt, in that chest-pressing suffocating way, and Brie didn't know how to fix anything. She didn't know how to get back to a place where she was excited to be home in the afternoons with her mom, watching soap operas on TV, and where she knew her dad would always do anything for her.

She also kept waiting for her dad to tell her mom about her kiss with Kennedy . . . but she didn't think he ever did.

He must not have, since nothing changed.

17.

THE YOUNG AND THE RESTLESS,
March 2006: Lily Winters almost has it all—her parents are back together, she has a new foster brother, school is going well. Then she falls for Daniel, a boy her mother forbids her to see. Lily doesn't want to hurt her mom, so she lies and sneaks around to be with Daniel. She almost pulls it off, too. Almost.

Come Monday, Brie was ready, again, to get back to school. She and Parker volunteered to keep Wallace—who was still on crutches—company during gym class. They sat on the stage at the back of the gymnasium, Parker swinging her legs off the edge while Brie and Wallace lay on their backs, the rest of their gym class playing a game of speedball in front of them.

"Gym class makes me hungry," Parker said.

"You aren't even doing anything," Brie replied.

"I know where they keep the Communion hosts back here," Wallace added. "They're in the cabinet behind the curtain." That's where they kept all the church stuff when the gym was used as a gym instead of as a church.

Parker frowned. "I don't think you're allowed to eat those."

"They aren't consecrated," Brie pointed out. "So I think it's okay."

"They taste like cardboard anyway, though. Not really worth the possible sin," Parker said. Brie and Wallace both agreed.

"How about the wine?" Wallace asked.

Brie laughed. "That I *know* would be a sin."

"Hey, guys!" The three of them looked down to find Kennedy standing below the stage, gazing up at them. Her hair was in a ponytail, which was half falling out since she'd been running around the gym. Parker shot Brie a look, and Brie tried to ignore it, feeling the heat in her cheeks.

She hadn't spoken to Kennedy since, well, since they'd kissed. Kennedy hadn't texted at all that weekend. Though in fairness, Brie hadn't reached out, either.

She could honest to God feel how awkwardly strained her own smile was.

Wallace, thankfully, was completely oblivious. "Hey, are you guys winning? I lost track."

Kennedy cringed. "I actually have no idea. I hate gym class."

"It's almost over," Parker said, pointing to the clock on the wall.

Brie just kept nervously smiling.

So, of course, the conversation came to a lull, because what on earth was she supposed to say? It didn't help that Parker elbowed her, and when Brie glared at her, Parker just elbowed her again.

As if Parker ever knew what to say when a crush gave *her* any attention. Brie was tempted to ask if she still had Jack Thomas's stick of gum saved somewhere.

The bell rang, and Parker, of course, was the first to speak again. "I'll help Wallace. You two go on ahead," she said. She gave Brie a not-so-subtle wink. Brie wanted to die a little.

She hopped down off the stage to stand beside Kennedy. "Want me to wait at the locker room for you?" Her cheeks immediately burst into flame, thinking about the last time they had been in the dressing room alone. "Or, I mean, we have next period together, so I could just find you then or whatever."

"Oh, um. Whatever you want," Kennedy replied.

So Brie followed Kennedy to the locker room and hovered quietly at the door as she waited for Kennedy to change from her gym clothes back into her uniform. She wasn't really sure what she was going to say. Should she bring up the kiss? Should she ignore it completely? Should she ask if Kennedy had told anyone, like Brie had told her dad, and how that had gone? Had it been good or weird or terrible?

Or should she just ask if Kennedy thought she did well on Mr. Strobel's science quiz?

When Kennedy emerged, freshly dressed in her uniform, her hair back down and hanging long against her shoulders, she smiled at Brie. Brie said nothing.

They followed the rest of their class back to their homeroom, but when Kennedy stopped walking just outside the doorway, Brie stopped to linger with her. "So," Kennedy said.

"So," Brie replied, and then, in one breath as if it were all one word, said, "Doyoulikegirls?"

"Oh, I—I, um," Kennedy stammered.

Brie took a deep breath. "I mean, I'm trying to say, if you aren't . . . if you don't . . . like, that's okay. I get it," Brie said with a shrug, even though she didn't really get any of it.

Kennedy bit her lip, glancing into their homeroom, which they were about to be late for, and then back at Brie. "I do," she said, her voice quiet. "I mean, I think. I mean . . ." She shook her head. "This is all a little confusing."

Brie sighed. "Yeah, tell me about it."

The late bell rang. Neither girl moved to head in.

"Do you want to maybe come over this week?" Kennedy asked.

Brie exhaled into a smile. "Yeah. I'd like that."

"Great," Kennedy said, her face lighting up.

They made their way into the classroom, and Brie thought for once that the butterflies in her stomach felt good instead of feeling like they were going to kill her from the inside out. Wallace asked if he could borrow a pen, and she lent him one as Mrs. Dwek asked them all to settle down. "We have an announcement that's going to happen in a few moments," she said. "So just stay in your seats and be patient."

They weren't very patient. Nor very quiet. Which didn't please Mrs. Dwek, especially when Shaun threw a pencil across the room and nearly hit Deena in the face. "What did I say!" Mrs. Dwek was starting to scold them, but they were all saved by the loudspeaker as it began to crackle like it did before every announcement.

"Attention, everyone." It was Sister Patricia, and the butterflies in Brie's stomach started moving faster, because it wasn't yet time to pray, and Sister Patricia came on the loudspeaker only for news related to religious events. "I have some news to announce. As you all know, the May Crowning is steadily approaching, and after much delibera-tion, we are pleased to announce who is going to do the honors."

Brie sucked in her breath and held it as she gripped the edges of her desk tightly. Wallace leaned over to say some-thing, but she quickly shushed him. She needed this not to be interrupted.

Oh God, what if it was her?

"All of the essays were very well done, and it was a hard decision, but one essay stood out among the rest."

Oh God, what if it wasn't?

"Your eighth grader chosen to crown Mary is . . . Kennedy Bishop!"

Brie released a *whoosh* of air, feeling that pulling, sinking feeling she was becoming all too accustomed to. The rest of the class gave its half-hearted applause as Mrs. Dwek gave her own congratulations. "Well done, Kennedy. We are very excited to hear you read your essay."

That was it, then. All the hard work and lies came down to this: Brie had *not* been chosen to crown Mary. Months had gone by since she'd told her mom she would be the one to do it, and Brie had worked so stupid hard. She'd done her homework. She'd studied. She'd listened in class and taken notes. She'd poured her heart out and she'd been honest and Ms. Santos had said she was brave, but really she was just . . . nowhere closer to cleaning up any mess, not the one at home or the one in her head, not any of it.

Wallace huffed. "Told you it would be someone like Kennedy."

Of course it was Kennedy. *Of course* it was.

Brie had lost. All the hoping and praying and *trying*, and she'd lost.

Mrs. Dwek kept talking, and Brie wanted her to just *shut up*. "I think you'll all really like Kennedy's essay. Would you like to tell them about it, Kennedy?"

Kennedy was blushing sheepishly, but she also looked happy and bright, and Brie felt a familiar bubble building up in her chest. She gripped the desk even more tightly, her knuckles turning white.

"Um." Kennedy bit her lip. "Well, I wrote about how it's so easy to feel separated from faith and religion sometimes. How, like, with school and friends and cell phones, it's easy to kind of feel detached from it. And how I'd just really like to get to know Mary. And how I'd like her to get to know me, and to find that special connection."

"Typical," Wallace mumbled. "Of course Kennedy comes up with something totally perfect."

But Brie wasn't listening to him. Not when the bubble in her stomach was ready to burst, because *she* had come up with that topic, not Kennedy. *She* was the one struggling with that. *She* was the one who was steadily beginning to hate that pendant around her mom's neck, and she was the one who sat in church trying to feel something other than shame, and she was the one who'd confided in Kennedy about all of it.

She was the one who'd given Kennedy the idea that had made her win.

Brie's eyes met Kennedy's, and Kennedy's smile faded, and Brie felt good about that. It meant that Kennedy knew. She knew Brie needed this, knew that she wouldn't have even had such a great topic if not for Brie. She *knew*.

The classroom felt suffocating. Brie shot her hand up in the air. "Mrs. Dwek, I need to go to the bathroom."

She barely waited for Mrs. Dwek to give her permission before she was up and out of her seat, leaving the room, ignoring the way she heard Kennedy say her name as she went by her, ignoring everything until she got into the bathroom and into a stall.

She balled her fists up and brought them to her eyes, willing herself not to cry.

Brie didn't know how her mom would react, but she knew that any hope she had of reconciliation was officially ruined.

May

Two Sundays until
the May Crowning

18.

GENERAL HOSPITAL, January 2008:
Maxie Jones lashes out at her mom for being an absent parent. She asks Felicia where she was when Maxie needed her the most. They fight a lot. I guess they don't know how to talk to each other.

Her parents were fighting. Brie didn't know what it was about. She was upstairs changing out of her school uniform when it started. She crept down the stairs as quietly as possible, in a tank top and sweatpants, and sat out of sight against the railing, doing her best to overhear.

"You went behind my back, the two of you," her mom was saying.

"That's not what this was," her dad replied.

"No? Then what was it?" Brie's mom argued. "Would you even have told me if I didn't see it on the credit card statement?"

"Of course I would have, but come on, Erin. I didn't see the harm. She wants to audition. It doesn't mean she'll get in."

"And if she does?"

"We'll go from there, then."

This was about her. Her dad had helped her fill out the MCPA application—obviously without telling her mom. Brie moved down another step, hoping to hear better.

"We can't afford it! I'm exhausted, Phil. *You're* exhausted. We're working our asses off, and she's got these grand plans that, frankly, would make things harder. You know that as well as I do," her mom said.

"We'd figure things out. That's what we do."

"I love you and your optimism, but things are just . . . not going how I planned. How we planned. Everything feels so out of control, and I don't know how to navigate any of this with her," her mom said. "Our entire relationship feels like it's changing, and I don't know how to just . . . hold on to her anymore."

Brie gripped the banister, pressing her head against the railing. Part of her wanted to stop this argument. She wasn't sure it mattered anymore. Not when Nico didn't even get in. Not when she couldn't even get a lead in her eighth-grade play. Not when her mom was bound to find out sooner or later that she wasn't really crowning Mary.

Not when she didn't know how to hold on to anything anymore, either.

"There's . . . a lot going on with her," her dad said.

Her stomach hurt. *Again*. Was he going to tell her mom about Kennedy?

"When are the auditions?" her mom asked. Brie wondered how much she'd popped up in her mom's prayers lately. If she'd been sitting in church in that intimate way, kneeling with her eyes closed and holding her necklace, thinking something like *Dear God and Mary and whoever is listening, please change my daughter back to normal.*

Brie wasn't even sure she'd blame her mom if she had been.

"They're in a few weeks. One of us will have to take her," her dad replied.

Her mom sighed, deep and heavy. "Okay. We'll let her do this. But *you* have to be the one to tell her that this doesn't mean we're agreeing to her attending this school. I don't want her to think I'm trying to keep her from being happy. I'm tired of being the bad guy."

"You're not the bad guy," her dad said. "But I'll do that if you yell at Trevor to stop ruining my grass. I'm *this close* to burying his car keys in the holes he's made on the lawn."

"I'm tired, Phil."

"I know. I'm sorry. Me too."

Brie heard them kiss. End of fight. End of conversation. She was allowed to audition after all.

At least, as of right now. MCPA auditions were at the end of May.

After the May Crowning.

Brie's phone buzzed, and she quickly reached for it so that her mom and dad wouldn't hear it and know she'd been listening. She pulled it out of her pocket, figuring it was Parker wanting to chat or Wallace asking what the homework was. She frowned when she saw it was Kennedy.

Kennedy, who'd been chosen to crown Mary, because she'd used one of Brie's ideas. Kennedy, who was the type of kid any parent would be proud of. Kennedy, who succeeded where Brie failed.

Kennedy, who was so infuriatingly, perfectly Brie's type.

Brie didn't even read the text message; she just clicked on it so the notification would go away.

Brie didn't know if the decision would last, but she'd heard her mom agree to let Brie audition for performing arts high school. "Trevor, can you drive me to the library?" Brie asked. She was sitting at the kitchen table with her homework when Trevor came in to scour the fridge for something to eat. Their mom was at work, and their dad was sleeping.

He pulled out the leftover chicken Brie had worked so hard to make the night before, and he threw it in the microwave. "I'm not allowed to drive you."

"Come on," Brie huffed. "No one will even know. It's just around the corner, and it's a stupid rule anyway."

Trevor shrugged, which usually meant he agreed. Or disagreed. This time Brie considered it agreement.

"Please, I need to do something for school," Brie said. The truth was, she needed to look up monologues. She wasn't ready to give up on MCPA just yet, and there was no way she felt safe Googling *anything* at home these days. "I'll tell Mom Parker's mom took us, and I'll text Mom or Dad to pick me up."

Trevor threw his head back and groaned. "Ugh, fine. Let me eat first."

They managed to make it to the library without dying, though Trevor barely waited long enough for her to exit the car before speeding away. The library was pretty busy, but Brie had to wait only a few minutes before a computer opened up. She'd brought the notebook she'd just started using to write down all the monologues she had watched for her school-play audition. She was hoping to find more, to find better. She needed something impressive—especially since her only theater credit was Grumpy.

Her phone buzzed, and she put it on silent. That was a library rule, right? It was a poor excuse for ignoring Kennedy, but Brie wasn't ready to face her yet.

She pulled up a browser and searched for good audition monologues, but she wasn't actually sure what to look for.

Could she still use a soap scene? *Should* she? She hadn't stopped thinking about Bianca Montgomery and Erica Kane and their scene from *All My Children* that had set her on a path to understanding herself a little better, a path that had led to her mom discovering all the things about Brie that still went unsaid between them.

I want you to see who I am, Mother. Can you see who I am? Can you? I'm trying to show you.

Brie wanted to know what happened next. She wanted to know where Erica and Bianca's relationship went after their fight. If they were okay—and if they weren't, if they ever came close to being what they used to be for each other.

How do soap opera mothers and daughters deal with things when they go wrong?

She pulled up YouTube. Typed into the search bar. Started a new list.

After an hour of searching, her head hurt, and still she had no monologue.

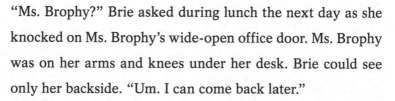

"Ms. Brophy?" Brie asked during lunch the next day as she knocked on Ms. Brophy's wide-open office door. Ms. Brophy was on her arms and knees under her desk. Brie could see only her backside. "Um. I can come back later."

Ms. Brophy banged her head on the desk as she quickly sat back on her heels. "Oh! Come in, Brie, come in. I'm just searching for an earring I lost. These are my favorites, but they dangle right off sometimes!" The earring that was still in Ms. Brophy's ear looked like a peacock feather. Brie, who was currently sporting a pair of big bright-purple hoops that clashed with her uniform, loved it. "Would you mind helping me? We can talk about whatever you came to talk about while we search!"

"Oh, yeah. Okay. Sure." Brie crouched down to help Ms. Brophy look. As much as she liked Ms. Brophy's earrings, she had no intention of crawling around on the floor. "I, uh, just wanted to ask you about my audition. For the play."

"Ah, yes. 'The Slut of Springfield.'"

Brie smiled. At least she was memorable. "I was kind of hoping you could tell me what I did wrong."

Ms. Brophy got off the floor, sat down at her desk, and motioned for Brie to take a seat on the folding chair she kept next to it. "What makes you think you did something wrong?"

"Well, I wasn't cast as a lead."

"That doesn't mean you didn't do well. A play is made up of a number of different important parts. Leads, supporting cast, even ensemble."

Brie tried not to audibly sigh. "I want to be an actress. I've been waiting for the eighth-grade play since, like, the fourth grade. I'm auditioning for MCPA at the end of the month, and I really want to get in, but I don't even know if I stand a chance of getting in. I mean, I thought maybe I did. But I've thought that about a lot of things lately that haven't come true. Or that got all messed up, but . . . Anyway, I was kind of hoping you had some advice, I guess."

Ms. Brophy smiled so big, Brie thought it must hurt. "I had no idea. You should have told me! I'm glad you're telling me now. You have such a presence about you—I think it's wonderful you're auditioning. Have you prepared a monologue yet?"

Brie shook her head. "I don't really know any good ones. Just, well, ones from soap operas. I like those a lot, but I kind of feel like maybe you and Ms. Santos didn't."

"I think you misunderstand," Ms. Brophy said. "We cast you as Grumpy because you were . . . well, you shocked us, really. It was so unexpected and, you know, hilarious."

Brie hadn't meant to be hilarious. She hung her head.

"No! No, that's a good thing, Brie. That's why you got Grumpy. Because you're so . . . energetic onstage! A real character actor," Ms. Brophy said.

"I don't understand."

"Deena is sweet, and your friend Parker, well, she was so miserable auditioning. The scowl on her face was just perfect as the Evil Queen," Ms. Brophy explained. "My point is, you were cast because you earned that role. You were perfect for it. Not because you weren't good enough to be someone else."

"Oh," Brie said, mulling it over. A colorful feather caught her eye, wedged between the wheel of Ms. Brophy's desk chair and the desk itself. "There, your earring."

Ms. Brophy excitedly grabbed it, putting it back into her ear even though it had gathered dust off the floor. "Thank you, Brie! But now, tell me, what is it you like about your shows?"

"About soaps, you mean?"

"Yes, that! It's a little unusual for your age group, you know." Ms. Brophy laughed. "I watched *Passions* years ago. Most soaps have been canceled, though, right?"

Brie nodded. "My mom and I always watched together. She started watching when she was home pregnant with my brother, Trevor, and then with me, and it stuck. I guess it stuck with me, too."

"So you're emotionally connected, because of your mother," Ms. Brophy said, and she nodded as if she suddenly understood everything. "I think you should stick with that, then. Maybe not the one you performed for us, though. Emotional connections are good. You had such energy and passion when you did your audition for us, but *feeling* what you're saying is even better. You want to pick a scene that makes you feel something so your audience feels it, too. Think about growing up watching soaps with your mom. Think about what that means to you and how you can recreate that feeling onstage."

Brie felt herself blushing.

"And by the look on your face," Ms. Brophy said, "I'm going to assume you already know exactly what you should be using."

Brie was *not* going to use that scene. No way. Absolutely not. Full stop.

Parker was no help in keeping her mind off crushes and coming out and everything else. "What's going on with you and Kennedy?" Parker was the queen of crushes. Brie should have known she would notice something was wrong straightaway.

Brie pulled a face, glancing around the classroom to see if anyone was listening. Wallace, who was right next to her, was luckily deep in conversation with Chris about baseball. "Shh. You're being loud. Nothing's going on."

Parker saw right through her. "Uh-oh. That was short lived."

Brie scoffed. "Your crushes are always short lived. Cut me some slack."

"Hey, quiet down, guys," Ms. Santos said as she pulled a stack of graded tests out of her bag. "I'm gonna pass your tests back, but keep it down while I do. Start looking at the next chapter in your textbook."

It was hard to keep quiet when Parker kept turning around to whisper to her, rustling the papers on her desk and bumping into the backpack beside her every time she did. At least it was one of those days when no one in class was actually being all that well-behaved. "I think I like Jack Thomas again," Parker whispered, making Brie clench her teeth. "I think he might be the one. I might ask him to dance at the graduation dinner dance."

"That's not for like another month. You'll change your mind at least four times by then."

"Maybe. Is that what happened to you? Did you change your mind about Kennedy?"

"Come on, you two, hush up," Ms. Santos interrupted, dropping Brie's test facedown on her desk. She tapped her finger on it. "I'm not super pleased with this grade, Brie."

Brie drooped back in her seat. She hadn't exactly studied for it.

"Hey." Ms. Santos tapped on the desk again, getting Brie to look up at her. "What's going on?"

"Nothing."

Ms. Santos was frowning. Brie had to look away from her, but she knelt down next to Brie's desk, too close for Brie's comfort. She smelled nice, not unlike Brie's mom's favorite lavender perfume, and Brie breathed through her mouth instead.

"What's going on, Brie?"

She wasn't going to have this conversation here. Not when Parker was still looking at her, and Wallace was next to her, nosy as always. Not when Shaun was making faces at her three rows over, assuming she was in trouble. Not when she didn't even know what to say. "Nothing, Ms. Santos. I'll do better next time."

Ms. Santos didn't reply, but she didn't move away, either. She kept looking at Brie, with that frown still on her face, and Brie looked back away. She flipped over the corner of the test. A big red 64 percent stared back at her.

Ms. Santos finally conceded and moved on to the next row. Brie could breathe better without her lavender perfume in her nose.

Parker leaned back over. "Is it because of the May Crowning?"

"Is *what* because of the May Crowning?" Brie said, as if she didn't know exactly what Parker was asking.

Parker rolled her eyes. "Just tell me! Do you still like Kennedy?"

Brie kept her eyes on her toes. She shrugged.

"Brie . . ."

"You change your mind all the time!" Brie practically shouted.

"Hey! Cool it, guys. I'm serious," Ms. Santos called from across the room. "Don't make me move one of you out into the hall."

That was enough to make Parker turn bright pink and face forward in her seat. Conversation over.

Or so Brie thought.

"You had a crush on *Kennedy*?" Wallace whispered to her.

Brie gritted her teeth and closed her eyes. She was ready to just go home.

***

Of course, when she got home, her mom was at work. Again. Brie hadn't watched *General Hospital* in what felt like forever, so she bypassed the living room and instead went up to her room. She didn't feel much like cooking for her dad and Trevor again, either. If she had to learn, so should they. Or at the very least, they were capable of picking up a phone and ordering their usual from Timoney's Pizzeria. She wondered how long she could stay in her room before someone dragged her out of it.

She looked at her cell phone. No notifications. Kennedy hadn't reached out to her in a few days. She supposed she deserved it if Kennedy gave up, but it still hurt to think about it.

She considered trying to find a monologue, but Ms. Brophy was in her head and so was Parker. She couldn't stop thinking about watching soaps with her mom and what it had felt like to stand on the hot-cocoa line at the ice rink with Kennedy, and remembering both of those things sucked.

Because she wanted so badly to experience those moments again, but they felt so far away.

Brie thought about the way she'd felt lately when she and her mom sat quietly in the living room, with all those things that went unsaid sitting between them. It made Brie feel like she'd swallowed rocks, and every day she and her mom spent not really talking, those rocks rolled around inside her.

She needed to think about something else. She needed to do—or fix—*something*.

The thought was enough to make Brie pick up her phone and scroll to Kennedy's name. Brie hadn't stopped being mad, but butterflies still flapped their wings against her stomach.

We should talk about it. She hit Send. Wondered how long it would take Kennedy to respond—if she'd respond at all.

Two seconds later, her phone buzzed: *Can you come over now?*

Brie talked Trevor into driving her, and she stood in front of Kennedy's door for almost an entire minute before she worked up the nerve to ring the doorbells. And use the knocker. She still wasn't sure which one she was *supposed* to use.

Kennedy answered almost immediately. She stood blocking the doorway, not creating enough space for Brie to step in. "Hi," Kennedy said.

"Hi," Brie replied and, when Kennedy didn't move, added, "Can I come in?"

Kennedy looked like she was thinking about the answer, and Brie wanted to remind her that she was the one who'd invited her over in the first place. But then Kennedy opened the door wider, and Brie stepped inside.

They went upstairs. Kennedy hovered by the door as Brie plopped herself in the middle of Kennedy's blanket-covered bed. Kennedy watched her carefully but said nothing, and Brie had the urge to ask her to take her hair out of the pony-tail she had it in.

Finally, Kennedy broke the silence to ask, "Are you mad at me?"

"No." Brie's exhale was shaky. "I don't know."

Her answer didn't seem to relax Kennedy, whose posture became only more rigid. "Well, I'm mad at you," she said.

"Yeah, I figured."

Kennedy lingered a little longer before closing her door and coming to sit with Brie on her bed. Brie was envious of the ease with which Kennedy shut the door, knowing that if the roles were reversed, Brie would spend the next however many minutes wondering what her mom would be thinking, what her mom would be feeling, and what her mom would do about it.

Kennedy twisted her fingers around the fringe on one of her blankets. "Why did you stop talking to me?" she asked.

Because you got chosen to crown Mary seemed like a stupid thing to say. Brie didn't know how else to explain it. "I lied to my mom," Brie said. "And you lied to me."

Kennedy was suddenly standing again. "I never lied to you!"

"You wrote your entire essay about something *I* said, without telling me!"

"It had nothing to do with you!" Kennedy took a deep breath, and when she spoke again, her voice was lower. "What you said that day about Mary . . . I *told* you I understood. Because I do—I understand, because my parents are super religious, too, and I don't know how I feel about it, either. And it all made me think about how no one really knows who I am or how I feel, and maybe I don't know, either, but that's what I wrote about. I didn't steal your idea, Brie, and I didn't lie to you. It was *my* essay, and it was about *me*."

Brie hadn't thought about any of that. She hadn't really thought about what Kennedy felt at all.

She bit the inside of her cheek, trying to keep herself from crying. She could feel it in her throat. "I told my mom I was chosen for the May Crowning. Like, *months* ago. And, well, obviously I wasn't."

"But . . . why? It's not like you . . ." Kennedy drifted off, cringing.

Brie wanted to scowl but didn't think she had an actual leg to stand on. "It's not like I really stood a chance?"

"That's not what I meant."

"I got caught looking at boobs," Brie blurted out. Kennedy's eyes opened comedically wide. Brie groaned, falling back onto Kennedy's bed. She stared at the ceiling. It was easier than looking at Kennedy. "She walked in on me while I was looking at pictures of a soap actress I really like. I didn't know she had naked photos, but she did, and I kept looking and my mom walked in. I needed to distract her, and I knew that would work, so I just . . . said it."

"Oh," Kennedy said.

"And it doesn't even matter, because she found out anyway. And I feel like I'm in so much trouble, but I didn't actually get in any trouble. My mom barely looks at me now, and my dad said he understood, but then I told him we kissed and he's being weird now, too, and I just . . ." She closed her eyes tight, because they were wet, and she didn't want Kennedy to see that. "I thought crowning Mary would make things better. It would have. I needed it to. And now it can't, because they chose you."

Kennedy didn't respond, so Brie sat up to look at her. Her eyes were glossy, and she was biting the inside of her cheek, too. "I'm sorry. About your mom and everything," Kennedy said. "I understand, really. Really, really, I do. But I'm still . . ."

"Mad at me?"

Kennedy hung her head. "I thought you didn't like me anymore. Like it was before the hockey game . . . when you used to, or you didn't . . ." A silence settled over them before Kennedy met Brie's gaze again to ask, "*Do* you like me?"

Something inside Brie's chest squeezed tight, making it difficult to breathe, even more difficult to admit her feelings.

Maybe her hesitation was all Kennedy needed to hear. "I think you should go," she said.

Even though she felt like maybe she should argue, Brie didn't want to. She didn't know how else this conversation could go. "Okay," she said. Then she called Trevor.

19.

ALL MY CHILDREN, September 2003:
Bianca is attacked, and in the aftermath wants to
confide in her uncle Jack. He's like a father to her,
and she's afraid to tell him. He tells her that she
can tell him anything. I wonder how many adults
mean it when they say that.

They got into a car accident on the way home, and really, Brie should have seen it coming.

The front of Trevor's old car was dented, and Trevor couldn't stop shaking, but otherwise they were okay. Trevor had a stop sign, and he *did* stop, but not long enough to avoid the oncoming truck. The truck was barely scratched. Brie made a mental note to buy a big car when she got the chance.

The police came, and Trevor gave them his license and registration and insurance card, and Brie sat in the car and tried to call their parents. She couldn't get a hold of her mom at work, and her dad wasn't answering at home. "I think Dad's sleeping," she told Trevor.

Trevor was still shaking. "Keep calling until he wakes the hell up," he said through his teeth.

After Brie had spent about a half hour trying to reach their parents, the cop gave them an escort home. Trevor's car was banged up but still drivable, and they didn't have far to go. When they got there, Trevor slammed the front door hard behind them. Their mom still wasn't home.

"What happened?" their dad asked, clearly drawn out of his bedroom by the commotion. He looked back and forth between the two of them, at Trevor's unsteady demeanor and angry eyes, and Brie's wet face. "*What happened?*" he asked again, this time more alarmed.

"I had to drive Brie to her girlfriend's house and we crashed the car and no one knows how to answer a goddamn phone!" screamed Trevor.

Brie flinched. Trevor never got this upset.

"You crashed the car? Are you okay? I've told you a thousand times you need to be more careful behind the wheel, Trevor!" Her dad took the stairs two at a time to meet them at the bottom, but Trevor pushed past him—hard— and stomped up the stairs to his room. "*Trevor!*" their dad shouted up the stairs as Trevor slammed his bedroom door closed.

Her dad rushed by her to open the front door to look out at the car, and Brie thought maybe the frantic look on his face would disappear when he saw it was only a fender bender, but it didn't. If anything, he looked worse when he turned back to face her. "Are you okay? You're not . . . Your mom doesn't want Trevor driving you anywhere!"

"It was important," Brie said. "I didn't think—"

"No, you didn't think. Jesus, Brie, I know your brother agreed to drive and that's on him, but you're not the only person in this family!"

Brie couldn't remember the last time her dad had shouted at her. She felt that familiar bubble, the one that had made her yell at Kennedy in class, that made her want to cry and scream all at once. "We were scared, Dad! We were scared, and you were sleeping!"

"Because I'm *tired*!" he shouted back and then stopped to take a deep breath, running his hands over his face before exhaling. "Just . . . go up to your room. Your mom will be here soon, and then we'll deal with all this."

Her dad went back to the door, going outside in only his socks and sweatpants and undershirt.

Brie stood in the middle of the quiet room alone.

✳

Her mom came home a half hour later. Brie was in bed. Trevor's room was also quiet, but she'd been able to hear the sounds coming from the living room and kitchen as her dad walked around and around, not once settling down, waiting for their mom to get home.

She heard her parents' loud but muffled voices. Heard their footsteps on the stairs. She rolled over to face the wall opposite her door. She closed her eyes, buried her head in her pillow, and burrowed under the blankets, trying to protect herself from hearing their argument with Trevor and the blame that would surely eventually be placed on her.

She must have fallen asleep, because the next thing she knew, she was opening her eyes and her mom was sitting on her bed, running a hand through Brie's hair. It felt nice. "Are you hurt at all?" Brie's mom asked.

Brie shook her head. "Dad's really, really mad," she said.

Her mom leaned down to kiss Brie's forehead. "He was scared, Brie. We have rules for a reason, and I don't want Trevor driving you, because you and he tend to be the worst distraction for one another, and Trevor gets distracted enough. That scares me, and it scared your father to come downstairs and see the two of you all disheveled and upset and not know why."

"We tried calling," Brie said. "No one answered."

"Which bothered him, too. He's running himself ragged right now. He's trying to make up for losing his job, and taking care of you guys and me, and he's just . . ."

"Tired?" Brie supplied. "That's what he said. I don't mean to be exhausting."

Her mom hummed in understanding, moving her hand to pat Brie's leg. "All right. Get some sleep. No Parker's house for a week, no plans this weekend. Okay?"

"Okay," Brie said. As far as punishments went, it wasn't so bad. "Hey, Mom?"

Her mom stopped before she reached the door, and turned back to Brie.

Brie swallowed the lump in her throat. "I don't mean to . . . I mean . . . is me auditioning for MCPA going to make Dad feel worse?"

"Brie . . ." Her mom stopped. "Your father wants you to audition. He knows it'll mean the world to you, and he wants that for you. And if you get in . . . well, we'll discuss it more then. Okay?"

Brie nodded her head. Her mom turned to leave, but Brie stopped her again. "Will you . . . will you be home to take me? To the audition, I mean. Can you be home to take me?"

Brie was tense with the certainty her mom would say no. That she would brush it aside like she'd brushed aside the MCPA play, like she'd brushed aside Brie's own performance. That work would have to come first. And after everything, could Brie even argue about it when she knew her dad was so tired and her mom was so stressed and work was so important?

But her mom took a deep breath and said, "I'll make sure I'm off."

It pushed at that yearning inside of Brie that had been tugging at her for months. Her voice sounded wobbly and desperate when she spoke again. "Mom?"

"Yes?"

"Trevor told Dad he drove me to my girlfriend's house, and I just wanted you to know she's not my girlfriend. I'm not, you know. I don't have a—"

"Brie," her mom interrupted. "Just get some sleep now, okay? We'll talk later."

Will we really? Do you promise me?

Her mom left, letting the door stay open a crack behind her, like she used to do when Brie was little.

Brie closed her eyes. She slept soundly all night.

20.

AS THE WORLD TURNS, June 2007:
Emily Stewart has been lying to her mother for
months because she's afraid that what she's
been doing is unforgivable. Her mom finds out
anyway—because they always do—in the worst
possible moment.

The eighth grade was gathered, rowdy and talking nonstop, in the auditorium to practice for the May Crowning. Kennedy sat in the front of the room, and Brie tried not to think about what dress Kennedy would wear for the Crowning or how pretty she would look in it.

"Hey!" Ms. Santos had lost all her patience. "If we have to remove any of you for talking, that's going to result in an immediate in-school suspension. Is that understood?" Usually Mrs. Dwek was the one to throw threats at them, but the eighth grade had been unruly for the past half hour, and nothing was getting done, and Brie was surprised it took Ms. Santos this long to get annoyed with them.

Brie sat back in her seat and stared at the big wooden cross that hung above the altar on top of the stage.

"My mom invited my grandparents to this thing," Wallace said. "So stupid."

Brie wasn't paying Wallace much attention. Instead, she watched as Ms. Santos led Kennedy to the statue of Mary. It was really pretty, and they used it only for this ceremony. Mary had a long blue-and-white dress and a hood that covered her dark-brown hair. Her arms were outstretched as she faced the eighth grade, looking down at them. Her eyes seemed kind.

Kennedy stood behind the statue of Mary, with a crown made of white and pink flowers in her hands. The focus was supposed to be on that halo of flowers, but Brie could look only at Kennedy.

Kennedy placed the crown on Mary's head, like Ms. Santos told her to, and the rest of the eighth grade started singing the song they had been practicing in chorus for weeks. *Gentle woman, quiet light, morning star, so strong and bright.* Kennedy's cheeks were bright pink, and she looked out at the rest of her class before her eyes met Brie's. They both quickly looked away.

Brie felt like she might throw up. She needed this entire event to just be over.

198

Afterward, the teachers sent the students to their home-rooms, but instead of following her classmates, Brie continued up the hall to knock on Ms. Brophy's door. She needed to talk to her and didn't want to lose her nerve. Besides, Ms. Brophy would write her a late pass if she asked. Ms. Brophy loved visitors.

"Hi, Ms. Brophy," Brie said as she knocked on the door.

"Hello again, Brie!" Ms. Brophy said. She was sketching away on a large pad of paper and had pencil smudges all up the side of her arm. "Here to talk more about your upcoming audition?"

"Actually, yeah," Brie said, taking a folded-up paper out of her skirt pocket. "I picked out a monologue. I was hoping you could help me."

She handed the wrinkled page to Ms. Brophy, but Ms. Brophy shook her head. "I'll gladly help you, Brie. But I don't want to read it. I want you to show me."

"Show it to you?"

"*Perform* it for me," Ms. Brophy said. "You want to act, I cannot help you unless you act."

Brie didn't like that. She'd thought maybe Ms. Brophy could just read it and know everything that Brie was trying to do and say without actually having to open her mouth. (Though she'd also been hoping that Ms. Brophy might just offer her a different monologue before Brie even started so she could chicken out entirely.)

Ms. Brophy wasn't stupid; there would be no going back after this.

Brie was sweating. But she took a deep breath and began.

She looked anywhere but at Ms. Brophy while she did it, while she said the words that had been swirling around in her head and twisting hard in her gut. When she finished, she clamped her sweaty hands together to try to stop them from shaking.

She kept her eyes on her feet, but when Ms. Brophy didn't say anything, she looked up to meet her gaze. Ms. Brophy's eyes were wet, and it startled Brie. "Oh, I, um. Should I do something else? I don't want to get in trouble. I just—"

"That was a powerful choice of a monologue," Ms. Brophy interrupted, wiping her cheeks.

"Oh," Brie said, her own eyes filling with tears the more she looked at Ms. Brophy's. "Really?"

"Yes. *Yes*. And you have my full support here, Brie." It was almost too much, both the tears and the kind words, and Brie held her breath to keep from crying. "Oh, sweetheart, it's okay. Come here." Ms. Brophy stood up and held out her arms, and Brie fell right into them, Ms. Brophy holding her almost too tightly. It felt good, though, not to have to use much of her own weight to keep herself standing.

Brie was not going to cry.

But also, she already was.

"It's good to bring all your emotions to the surface while acting, but I also know it's not easy," Ms. Brophy said.

Brie broke the hug to wipe her cheeks, feeling the embarrassed heat that flushed her face. "You think I stand a chance, then? For the auditions, I mean."

"I think you're going to be just fine." Ms. Brophy sat back down in her rolling desk chair, and it skidded a bit. "But that doesn't mean there aren't things here to work on, so listen up, because I've got some notes."

Good, Brie thought as she dried her face. She would focus on those notes.

It was hard to focus on anything related to her auditions, though, now that the May Crowning was finally here.

And Brie had yet to tell her parents that she'd lied.

It was now or never, as Brie's mom fussed over the dress she'd picked out for Brie without asking for Brie's opinion. It was pink and floral and itchy. Her brother was in khakis; her dad wore a tie. Her grandparents were downstairs in the living room.

But the words could not come out, because her chest and her throat were tight, and she could barely swallow, and really, she was kind of hoping for divine intervention.

"What shoes are you wearing?" her mom asked. Brie shrugged, which prompted her mom to dig through Brie's closet for a respectable pair. She found white strappy ones that Brie didn't even remember owning. "Here, try these."

Brie slipped them on. "Grandma and grandpa are downstairs?" she asked.

"Yes, and we really need to hurry up," her mom responded. "Do you want some makeup? I can give you some gloss and a little eye shadow if you want."

"No thanks," Brie said. She looked into the mirror, dress and shoes on, her hair down over her shoulders. Her mom came over to tuck the strands behind Brie's ears, making Brie blink back sudden tears.

What was she going to do? How on earth was she going to fix this?

"Actually, wait." Her mom reached behind her neck to unhook the clasp and gently, with reverence, pulled off her necklace. The one with her pendant of Mary, the one she never took off. "Here. I want you to wear this."

"What?" Brie's voice was high and scratchy as her mom draped it around Brie's tight throat. She swallowed hard, watching in the mirror as the pendant sat on her chest. The metal was cool to the touch, but still, Brie flinched as if it burned. "But it's yours."

Her mom made a sound of agreement through her lips. "It looks nice on you."

Brie tentatively brought a hand up to rub her fingers on the pendant, as she had seen her mom do over and over. She was hoping maybe it would give her strength, or whatever it did for her mom, but Brie felt nothing but metal. "Why's all this so important to you?" Brie found herself finally asking. Maybe there was a little strength in the necklace after all.

"The May Crowning?"

"All of it," Brie said, fingers still toying with the pendant.

"You know your grandfather wanted to be a priest," her mom said and then smiled. "Before he met your grandmother, that is. She sort of threw a wrench into all that."

"I know, but . . . is that all?" Brie asked. Because it seemed so simple when she put it like that, and if her mom felt so strongly just because *her* parents felt so strongly, why couldn't Brie just feel it, too?

"Well, no. Not really," her mom said. "My mom wasn't really religious when she met my dad. It was all kind of new to her, and, well, she wasn't exactly all that sure about it. You know how she is, so skeptical of everything. But she loved your grandfather and wanted to share this huge part of him. She ended up gravitating toward Mary. She really liked how, for the most part, Mary was the only woman in the room." Brie's mom smiled, a private, intimate smile that reminded Brie of her mom's demeanor in church. "Her love of Mary became mine."

Brie didn't really know what to say. "Oh."

Her mom placed her hand over Brie's, which was still holding on to the pendant. "I hope it becomes yours, too."

She wrapped her arms around Brie in an awkward sort of backward hug. "Though here you are, crowning Mary. So I guess something has stuck, huh? I'm so proud of you."

Which was exactly what Brie had been hoping for, right? Which was exactly why she'd lied.

Which was exactly why she couldn't just open her mouth and tell her mom the truth.

The auditorium/church was filled to capacity, except for the first five rows, which had been reserved for the eighth grade. They were lined up in the main hall, the boys on one side and the much longer girls' line on the other side, waiting.

They didn't wait all that quietly, and Brie was certain the entire church could hear Mrs. Dwek's loud shushes. Her family was somewhere in the auditorium, waiting patiently—with cell phone cameras already open—for Brie's special day.

Only it wasn't Brie's special day. It was Kennedy's. Kennedy, who stood at the very front of the procession in a white dress, the bottom of which was scattered with little blue flowers that matched the blue ribbon in her hair and the Mary statue's dress. The ribbon kept Kennedy's hair out of her face, and instead it fell on her shoulders in loose, bouncy curls that Brie wanted to gently tug on, just to see them bounce more. Kennedy's fingers were fidgeting with the hem of her dress, with the ribbon in her hair, with those curls, and Brie could tell that she was nervous.

Brie was nervous, too.

She was nervous because she still liked to look at Kennedy, and she missed Kennedy, and her mom was right inside the church, waiting for Brie to crown Mary, but Brie wouldn't be crowning Mary. Kennedy would be. Kennedy, whom her dad knew she'd kissed, whom Trevor called her girlfriend. And Brie's grandparents were there, and would they suddenly treat her differently, too, if they knew about her feelings and crushes just like her mom did? Just like her *dad* did?

Would Brie be able to answer the questions, any of them? The *Why did you say you were crowning Mary?* or the *Why do you keep looking at that girl?* or the *Are you gay, Brie? Are you thinking about girls the way you should be thinking about boys, in a church of all places?*

"Are you okay?" Wallace asked from his place beside her.

Her eyes were wet. The statue of Mary blurred as Brie looked up at it, and she was suddenly reaching for her mom's pendant before she dropped her hand to her side. She didn't want to be wearing that pendant. She didn't want the weight of it around her neck. Mary, the Mother of God, never had to be disappointed by *her* child. She knew exactly who he was from the start. She never had to look at him any differently, not like Brie's mom would when she realized Brie had lied.

Not like Brie's mom had when she'd realized Brie liked girls.

Hail Mary, Mother of God. Pray for us sinners.

Brie wasn't okay. She *was not* okay.

If this were a soap opera, one of Brie's shows, someone would come and interrupt the ceremony with some ludicrous reveal of some sinister plot, saving Brie from humiliation. Or no—if this were a soap, everything would come crashing down on Brie the moment she set foot in that auditorium. Dramatic lightning would strike, and accusations would fly, because she was the villain in all of this. She was the one in the wrong.

She was the one who had lied, the weight of her secrets too heavy on her shoulders, and she thought about her favorite soap characters, the drastic things they had done when caught in similar situations.

Brie closed her eyes tightly, and the voices around her, the shushes from Mrs. Dwek—everything was too loud as she fell to the floor.

Okay, so even Brie had to admit that it was a little dramatic. But at least she was now sitting on the front steps of the school, so she could "get some nice spring air," as Ms. Santos put it, and her mom paced back and forth, wondering out loud if she should take Brie to the hospital.

Brie hadn't really fainted. She'd sort of faked it, just to make everything stop. It had worked, for an all-too-brief moment. But now the eighth grade was proceeding into the church, and Brie was outside with Ms. Santos and her mom, too aware of her heartbeat in her neck, right under the pendant she wanted to take off.

"How are you feeling now?" her mom said. "Can you go back in there? They need you in there."

Brie felt Ms. Santos's eyes on her. She avoided looking at them.

She put her head between her knees, hoping maybe she would just throw up and feel a little better and get out of having to tell the truth. But nothing happened, so she muttered into her knees, "I lied."

At least the ground didn't open up and swallow her whole.

"What?" her mom asked. Ms. Santos stayed quiet. Brie had a feeling Ms. Santos was starting to put all the pieces together.

"I'm not crowning Mary."

"What?" her mom said again. "I don't understand. Why not? What did you do?"

Brie looked up. "Nothing. I was never supposed to crown Mary. I wasn't chosen. I lost. It was never me. It was always Kennedy."

Her mom just stared at her. Ms. Santos tried to intervene: "I didn't know Brie lied to you, Mrs. Hutchens, but I do know crowning Mary was very important to her. She did really well on her essay."

"Get in the car," her mom interrupted.

"What?" Brie asked. "But we have the mass. Grandma and Grandpa and Dad are all inside."

"Get in the car, Gabrielle. *Now*."

Brie got up so quickly, she almost passed out for real.

They left a confused Ms. Santos by the front of the school while the rest of their family was still inside the auditorium. Brie would have felt like she was being kidnapped if she hadn't been with her mom. Not for the first time, she thought very seriously about opening the door of a moving car and jumping out.

Brie's only concern was how much that would hurt. She was hurting enough already.

Her mom had a tight grip on the steering wheel and kept her eyes on the road. The radio wasn't on, and the silence made Brie feel as though she were being driven to her execution.

But they were just driving home. They pulled into the driveway, and her mom turned off the car and got out, still silent, slamming the driver's-side door behind her. Brie stayed in the car, watching her mom as she walked up to their porch and into their house. Brie couldn't hear if she slammed that door, too, but she would have bet money on it.

She couldn't sit in the car forever. She opened her door to head inside.

Her mom was in the kitchen with a glass of water. "Mom?" Brie prompted, eager to get this over with. She'd been sitting with it for months, and now her mom knew the truth, and Brie wanted to just skip to the part where everything was out in the open and she was sent to her room without dinner.

She wanted it over. Finally and truly over.

"Mom?" she said again.

"Why would you . . . ?" Her mom stopped, put the glass of water down. "Why on earth would you lie about this? Why would you let us . . . *celebrate* you? Why would you let me tell your grandparents, and why would you keep this up for months, knowing we would have to find out the truth eventually?" She was shouting by the time she got to the end.

"I don't know," Brie said.

"No. No, no, no. You're going to have to do better than that," her mom said. "Tell me why."

"Dad's not going to know where we are."

"*Why*, Gabrielle?"

Think of something to say. Think of it quickly. "It distracted you?"

"Distracted me? From *what*? What the hell is going on with you lately? I hardly recognize you anymore!"

And that hit Brie the hardest. Her mom didn't recognize her and hadn't been able to ever since Brie had started figuring out exactly who she was. It was confusing, sure, but she was still *Brie*, and her mom could not see that. "Because you're not trying! You don't recognize me because you're not trying to know me!"

"Don't raise your voice."

"I lied because I was scared, and I wanted you to like me!" Brie kept shouting anyway. "And you made everything harder. I tried so hard to make it happen because I wanted to do this for you. I wanted you to just *talk* to me!"

"Do not blame this on me—"

"I know you read all that stuff on my computer," Brie said. "I *know* you did."

Her mom reached for the necklace that wasn't around her neck. "This is about you lying and causing a scene this afternoon."

"Why won't you talk to me about it?" Brie asked, her nose burning as tears spilled from her eyes, no matter how hard she tried to keep them in. "Why do you keep not talking to me about it?"

"What do you want me to say, Brie?" her mom said, her own eyes full of tears. "What *exactly* do you want me to say?"

That you love me. That it's okay.

"I need to get in touch with your father so he knows what's going on and doesn't panic," her mom said instead. "Go to your room. I can't look at you anymore right now."

"You can't look at me ever."

"*Now*, Brie."

"I like girls, Mom! I like Kennedy!"

"Get upstairs now!" Her mom screamed so loud it echoed throughout the empty house, vibrating in Brie's ears and stunning her silent. More tears slipped down Brie's face, and she realized that her mom's cheeks were wet, too.

Her mom took a deep breath. "Brie . . ." she said, but Brie didn't want to listen to her anymore. She pulled hard at the necklace around her neck, and the clasp gave way, and Brie threw it across the kitchen at her mom. She turned to run up the stairs and into her bedroom—leaving her door open, because that was the new rule, wasn't it? Or was it only when she had girl friends over? She dove onto her bed, buried her face in her pillow, and sobbed.

21.

GENERAL HOSPITAL, February 1998:
Carly Benson reveals that she's Bobbie Spencer's daughter after purposely wreaking havoc on Bobbie's life. Bobbie is angry and calls Carly diabolical and relentless. There's a lot of anger. I have no idea how they got through this.

The rest of her family got home about an hour later, but no one came into Brie's room for another half hour. When the knock on her door finally came, she was surprised to see it was Trevor. "You okay?" he asked.

Brie shook her head and rolled away from him toward the wall.

"What was that all about, anyway?"

"Leave me alone, Trevor."

"I just wanted to let you know that Mom took Grandma and Grandpa home," he said. "So you're in the clear if you're hungry."

She *was* hungry. They'd had plans to get brunch after the ceremony, but that clearly would not be happening now. Trevor left to close himself up in his room again, and Brie got out of bed. She kicked off her strappy shoes and took off her scratchy dress, throwing on sweats instead. She left her feet bare and walked quietly down the stairs to the kitchen.

She'd just opened the fridge when she heard her dad clear his throat behind her. "I'm hungry," she said, not turning around to face him.

"Okay," he said simply.

She faced the refrigerator a moment longer before curiosity got the best of her. She closed it and turned to look at him. "Are you mad at me, too?"

"Want me to make you an omelet?" he asked. She nodded, and he crossed the room to reach above her to get the eggs out of the refrigerator. He took out a frying pan and began cracking the eggs. "I'm not mad. Confused, maybe."

"Are you mad that I kissed Kennedy at the school play?" Brie quietly asked as she pulled the cheese out of the refrigerator and handed it to him.

"Of course not," he said and then paused. "Okay, honestly, Brie? It made me uncomfortable. And I'm sorry."

She frowned. "Like how it made me uncomfortable to have you working at school?"

He shrugged, focusing on the eggs.

"I'm sorry, too," Brie admitted softly. "For making you feel bad about working there."

He turned and smiled at her. Brie couldn't help but smile back, even if both their smiles were kind of wobbly. "It doesn't matter to me who you . . . you know. You're growing up so fast, and I hate it. I think I might have reacted the same if she was a boy."

"Mom wouldn't," Brie said. "If Kennedy was a boy, none of this would have happened."

"Your mom loves you," he said as he added the cheese to the sizzling eggs. It smelled good. "And so do I. Your mom's dealing in her own way, but she *is* dealing. Give it time, like I needed time, too. Meanwhile, kid, you're still in trouble for today. No more lying, okay?"

He maneuvered the omelet onto a plate and handed it to her.

"Okay," she said—and she meant it. "No more lying."

Why was time necessary? How much time? Was it two weeks? Because that was how long Brie was grounded. The punishment was delivered by her dad, because her mom did not speak to her the rest of that Sunday.

So, as was the norm lately, Brie was relieved to be back in school the next day, away from her mom, even if sitting in Sister Patricia's classroom made her want to crawl under her desk and both Parker and Wallace were full of questions about what had happened to her yesterday. It was stressful wondering if Sister Patricia would ask her why she'd missed one of the most important events at OLPH, or if Ms. Santos had already told her. It was even more stressful to listen to Sister Patricia talk about how since they were graduating soon and some of them would be going to public school, their faith was going to have to be something they *decided* to continue with. They were going to have to decide what they wanted.

Brie didn't know what she wanted.

No, that wasn't true. She wanted to be allowed to audition for performing arts school, and she wanted to be allowed to crush on Kennedy, and she wanted her mom to be the one to say, "Yes, both of those things are okay."

Brie felt disconnected from her faith and disconnected from her mom, and was that all because she was gay?

"Kennedy's not here today. Her parents must have been nice enough to let her take off after yesterday," Parker turned around to whisper to Brie. "She looked so pretty when she was crowning Mary."

"Turn around, Parker," Brie grumbled.

"I'm just saying."

"Well, don't."

Parker took another breath, but Brie cut her off before she could say anything else about Kennedy or crushes or boys. "I don't want to talk about whoever you're crushing on this hour, either, Parker! It's annoying!"

Parker's face flushed immediately. "Fine," she mumbled and turned back around.

Great, Brie thought. *Add Parker to the list of people I've messed things up with.*

"I didn't mean to . . . I'm sorry, Parker," Brie whispered, leaning forward, but Parker did not turn back around. Brie kept talking. "Everything's just been so messed up lately. And I know I shouldn't have snapped at you because of it, but it's just hard sometimes to listen to you talk about boys. I don't feel comfortable talking about . . . Anyway, my mom's been so . . . I don't know."

Parker still did not turn around, but Parker never ignored anyone. Brie knew she was listening, and the more Brie said, the easier it was to breathe. "We have to pray every single day, you know? I go to church every single week. Twice, because my mom makes us go on Sundays, too, and what if that's not okay? *Is* it okay that I go to church? I mean, how am I supposed to connect with my mom through her faith if I don't even know . . ."

"Oh, Brie." Parker's voice was soft when she finally turned around.

Brie shook her head. There really wasn't much more to say.

No, that wasn't true. Because she found herself admitting, to the one person she knew she could always admit crush-related things to, "I miss Kennedy."

"Then you should tell her that," Parker said and then smiled. Brie loved that smile. It was a *we are best friends, so you are forgiven* smile. "I'm still rooting for you two."

"Parker? Brie? Why do I hear voices back there?" Sister Patricia interrupted, successfully ending any and all conversation.

But once Sister Patricia wasn't focused on them anymore, Brie carefully pulled out her cell phone, hiding it in the pleats of her skirt. She scrolled to Kennedy's name, something she had not done in too long.

Parker was right. Brie needed to try to fix this.

Missing you at school today, she texted. And then added, *There's no one to answer all of Mrs. Dwek's questions. Students are being called on randomly. It's awful for those of us who are terrible at math!*

There was no response. Brie, if she was being honest, didn't really expect there to be.

But near the end of the last period, Brie's phone buzzed, startling her. She quickly pulled it out of her pocket.

There were just three words. They made Brie want to punch the air.

Miss you, too.

In homeroom at the end of the day, Wallace leaned over to ask, "Do you think Parker likes me?" They were all sitting around waiting for the dismissal bell, bags packed and ready, Mrs. Dwek ignoring them from her desk. She'd surrendered to the fact that they wouldn't settle down.

"Parker likes everyone. Why, do *you* like Parker?" This was the last thing Brie wanted to be involved in, but considering the mood she'd been in when talking to Parker earlier, she owed it to her best friend to scope out the situation.

Wallace sighed. "No. I mean, she's fine, but she's my friend. The dinner dance is coming up, and I sort of wanted to have a date."

Brie would've liked to say she'd forgotten all about the dinner dance, but that wasn't true. Parker had been talking about it nonstop for weeks. Parker, like Wallace, wanted a date. Brie, well . . . It wasn't that Brie didn't want a date. It was just that she knew she wouldn't be able to have the date that she really wanted.

Some things were pretty black and white when it came to Catholic school.

Okay, so it wasn't totally OLPH's fault Kennedy still wasn't really talking to her.

"How about this," Brie said. "Unless you decide on someone else to ask, I'll go with you to the dance."

Wallace pulled a face. "I didn't think you liked me like that."

Brie pulled that same face. "I don't. But we can go as friends. Deal?"

Wallace tilted his head to the side and narrowed his eyes, thinking about it. But then he pressed his lips together and held out his hand. "Deal."

There was a knock at the door that barely cut through the sounds of eighth-grade chatter and gossip. Ms. Santos popped her head in. "Sorry to disturb, but I was hoping to catch Brie before dismissal." She met Brie's gaze. "Come see me after the bell. I already spoke with your dad. He'll be waiting for you."

"That doesn't sound good," Wallace muttered.

Brie didn't think so, either, but when the dismissal bell rang and everyone gathered their things to leave, she made her way to Ms. Santos's classroom. It was empty of students by the time she got there, but Ms. Santos was indeed waiting for her at her desk. She had a stack of papers on it, like she always did, and she was marking them. Brie knocked on the door. "Ms. Santos?"

She looked up and smiled. "Come have a seat, Brie."

Brie wasn't so sure she wanted to sit. She entered the classroom, choosing to hover in front of Ms. Santos's desk instead. "Am I in trouble?"

"I wanted to check in with you. About . . . yesterday," Ms. Santos said, and Brie felt her cheeks catch fire.

"You didn't tell anyone, did you? About what happened?"

"Of course not. That was clearly between you and your family, but it . . . gave me a lot of answers," Ms. Santos said. "It also gave me a lot more questions. What happened, Brie?"

"Noth—"

"What happened," Ms. Santos interrupted Brie's poor excuse, "to cause one of my best students this year to suddenly give up again?" She reached into her bag, pulling out papers that Brie recognized as the essays they'd had to turn in the other day. Brie had done hers in homeroom the morning it was due. The first paragraph had a lot of red penned notes, but they stopped there. There was no grade on the top. "I didn't even finish," Ms. Santos explained. "It was clearly a waste of both our time."

Brie suddenly felt like she might cry. "I'm sorry."

"Talk to me, Brie. I promise you can tell me anything."

Can I tell you that I had a crush on you? That I ended up with a crush on Kennedy? That my mom still won't look at me or talk to me?

There was a crucifix on the wall behind Ms. Santos's head, just like there was in every classroom. Brie felt the weight of that cross bearing down on her.

Ms. Santos followed her gaze. "Brie—"

"I like girls, Ms. Santos," Brie blurted. It seemed like in the movies or on TV, anytime a girl realized she liked girls, or a boy realized he liked boys, they had one big moment. One moment when they said the words and came out, and that was that, full stop. Brie felt like she had barely come out to herself yet, and still, *her moment* was happening at least once a week. Would this be her life now? Having to come out again and again and again? "My mom found out."

Ms. Santos's smile softened. "How's that been for you?"

Brie shook her head. She couldn't explain. The lump in her throat wouldn't let her. "I don't know why I thought crowning Mary would help. It probably wouldn't have made a difference. Would it have?"

"I don't know," Ms. Santos answered honestly. "And I'm really sorry things are hard for you right now. But—and forgive me for putting my teacher hat on right now—can I tell you what I do know?"

Brie nodded.

"I know that you are funny and smart, and when you're motivated, nothing can stand in your way," Ms. Santos said, pulling papers from the back of the pile. They were from a couple of months ago, when Brie had been trying to write the best essays she could. They were As. (Some Bs.) They were pretty good. "I know the May Crowning essay was the be-all and end-all for you. But I would just hate to see you lose what you've worked for. You did it, Brie. You worked hard and did it. And maybe you didn't get chosen—because sometimes we work hard and someone still earns it more—but you grew, and you were brave, and you were so good. Don't give up on me now."

"I'm tired of trying," Brie admitted.

Ms. Santos nodded. "It can be exhausting. But nothing changes if you stop."

"It'd be easier, though."

"Would it be?" Ms. Santos asked.

No. It wouldn't. It would just keep hurting.

"Take this essay back," Ms. Santos said, handing her the half-graded mess Brie had turned in. "Redo it. Write it like I know you can. I don't want to have to give you a crappy grade. Redo this essay, and I'll see what I can do."

Brie nodded. "Thank you, Ms. Santos."

Brie left her classroom feeling lighter. As though the weight of that cross had been lifted off her shoulders. She needed this second chance.

Later that week, her dad had a job interview.

The rest of the family waited for him in the living room, *General Hospital* on the TV, which for them to watch together was . . . new. Well, not new, but old and familiar in a way that made Brie ache. Trevor was taking up the entire love seat with his long body, asking a lot of stupid questions. ("Wait, she's married to who? I thought she was with that other guy." "Wait, that's *not* her baby?") It kept them focused on the TV and not the situation, at least.

Her dad got home right at the commercial break. His shirt was untucked, and his tie was loose. Brie's mom was the first off the couch. "How'd it go?" she asked.

He shrugged. "I'm going to go lie down a bit. Make sure I'm up by dinner, okay?"

He kept walking, but Brie's mom grabbed him by the arm and held tight. "Phil, wait, stop. Come on, let's talk about this. How'd it go?"

Her dad glanced at Brie and Trevor, who were both sitting ramrod straight on the couches, watching their parents. "It went, Erin. Just leave it at that, okay?"

"Not okay," she said, keeping her grip on him.

"They thanked me for my time but said that they were going to go in a different direction," he said. He looked around the room, keeping his eyes away from Brie and Trevor and even Brie's mom as she hugged him tight. "I can only guess that direction is *younger.*"

"You're not old," Brie said.

Trevor threw a pillow at her.

"What? He's not!"

"It's okay, Dad," Trevor said. "You'll kick ass at the next one."

Their dad chuckled, wrapping an arm loosely around their mom's waist. "Thanks, guys. Just, you know, feeling a little useless is all."

The way the three of them fell silent after he said that made Brie sure she wasn't the only one whose heart hurt at his admission. "Come sit with us," her mom said, tugging at his arm.

"Yeah," Brie said, moving over to make more room. "You can rest here, if you want. We won't bother you."

He conceded and let Brie's mom lead him to the couch, where he flopped down between her and Brie. Trevor stayed on the love seat, and they all settled in to watch the rest of the soap together. Brie leaned over to rest her head on her dad's shoulder as he closed his eyes and leaned his head against the back of the couch.

※

That night, Brie lay awake in her bed, unable to sleep. She turned down the brightness on her phone as much as she could and scrolled through it.

She hadn't texted Kennedy back, and her fingers hovered over her name. She clicked it, saw the *Miss you, too*, and decided to take another chance.

My dad had a job interview today. It didn't go well. I feel bad.

She hit Send.

Held her breath.

(Began breathing again when she could no longer hold it.)

After about five minutes, she sighed, figuring Kennedy was already in bed. She was about to put the phone down on her nightstand when it suddenly buzzed in her hand.

I'm sorry for your dad. Is he okay?

Brie sat up in bed, staring at her phone. Kennedy had responded! She was awake, and she had responded! Brie had to pick her words very carefully now to keep the conversation going.

I don't know. I hope so. I feel even worse though that I was so mean to him when school started.

She hit Send and waited a moment before adding, *I feel bad I was so mean to you too.*

When nothing else was forthcoming, Brie moved to put her phone on the dresser. She would keep trying. At least until Kennedy told her to stop.

22.

ONE LIFE TO LIVE, October 2001:
Viki Lord finds out that Natalie is her biological child, not Jessica. Still, Viki says almost immediately that it doesn't change how she feels, that Jessica is still every inch her daughter. No matter what.

"You're ready for this weekend, Brie," Ms. Brophy said. Brie wasn't sure she believed her. "Do you know what you're going to wear? You don't need to be too fancy or anything, but you should try and look nice."

"Uh, no. I didn't think about that," Brie said.

"I'm sure your mom will be more than happy to help," Ms. Brophy added.

Brie scowled. No one had so much as mentioned the audition for MCPA since before the May Crowning. Not even Brie, who was worried that if she brought it up, the bubble would burst and the uneasy silence between her and her mom would become something much worse. "I'll figure it out," she said.

"And make sure you're there at least fifteen minutes before your call time, okay? It's important to be prompt," Ms. Brophy continued.

Brie scowled more. She wasn't even sure who was taking her. Now she had to worry about being there early?

Which meant that when Brie got home, she had to ask. She sat in the living room with her mom, watching *General Hospital.* They hadn't *talked* about it, but they'd started watching again since the day of her dad's interview. Not that Brie was really watching—more like staring at the screen, trying to will the words out of her mouth to ask about the audition.

Maybe she should just wait and ask her dad.

"You feeling okay?" her mom finally asked. "You haven't said a single thing since you got home."

Brie honestly hadn't thought her mom would notice. They didn't really talk much these days, anyway. "I think I asked what was for dinner."

"Yeah, an hour ago."

Brie slouched against the couch and gave in. "The audition for MCPA is Saturday."

"Oh."

"Am I still going?"

Her mom got really quiet, and something inside Brie's chest squeezed tight at the possibility that she would say no, that Brie really wouldn't get to audition. Her mom's hand was resting against her chest. She hadn't worn her pendant since the day Brie had thrown it at her.

"We said you could," her mom finally said.

Brie didn't feel all that relieved. "So it's still okay?"

Her mom reached for the remote and turned off the TV, making the sinking feeling in Brie's stomach worse. "It's okay, but . . ."

Brie almost didn't want to ask. "What?"

"If you get in, it will be very, very hard for us to send you there."

Brie didn't understand. She already knew this. They'd already told her this, over and over, ever since she'd gotten the very first brochure. "I know."

"I mean, it would be extremely difficult, and your father, he would do anything, I mean anything, to send you there if it's what you tell him you want, and I just worry that—"

"Mom, I said I know," Brie interrupted. She chewed the inside of her cheek for a moment before adding, "I just want you to let me try."

Her mom nodded. "Okay."

She flipped the TV back on, but the show was over and the news was starting. Brie knew she should go do some homework before dinner—she still had to turn in her revised essay for Ms. Santos—but she wasn't able to leave yet. "Will you . . ."

"What's that?" her mom said, lowering the volume.

Brie took a deep breath. "Will you still take me? To the audition, I mean."

Her mom looked at her carefully, and Brie squirmed under her gaze. "Yeah," she said. "I'll still take you."

Brie texted Kennedy again the night before the audition. *Wish me luck*, it said. *Tomorrow's the big day.*

You'll do great, Kennedy responded. *What monologue are you using?*

Brie made her phone a bit brighter, wanting to make sure she didn't miss a second of conversation. *It's from a soap opera.*

Good, Kennedy texted. *Wish I could hear it.*

Just the idea of Kennedy watching her monologue made the butterflies in Brie's stomach flutter faster, their wings feeling more like rocks to her. *Maybe we can hang out after?*

The butterflies flew right out of her stomach the minute Kennedy responded, *Okay.*

With only a half hour left until the auditions, Brie was absolutely going to throw up. She lowered the car window to stick her head outside. "Stop that," her mom said. "You don't want your hair looking like a mess when we get there."

Brie slouched back and closed the window.

She was nervous but determined. She wasn't really thinking much about the judges and how they would decide whether attending MCPA was even something she would get to consider in the future. She just kept wondering where her mom would be during her audition. And what she would think when it was over.

No more lying, Brie thought. It's what she'd promised her dad, and she'd meant it.

They pulled into the parking lot of Monmouth County Performing Arts. Brie tried not to think about the last time she'd been here. She didn't want to think about how her mom had let her down. She didn't want to think about how soft Kennedy's hand had felt in her own as they'd sat in the auditorium.

Or maybe she did want to think about them both. Maybe she should.

Her mom turned off the car and faced Brie. "You ready?"

Brie thought that after all this time she would be. Now, though, she wasn't so sure.

The hallway was lined with folding chairs occupied by other potential students and their guardians. Some sat quietly; others rehearsed. Some said their lines softly to themselves; some loudly, as if they were in front of the judges.

Some looked pale and sweaty; others looked like they already knew they had a spot.

Brie was somewhere in between—not quite terrified, not quite confident—as she sat next to her mom in a cold gray folding chair, her shoulders straight, her eyes on the ceiling as she thought about why she was here and what she was about to do.

Ms. Brophy had helped her take an emotional and important scene that was a dialogue between two people and transform it so that Brie could perform it alone. "You say your lines like you're speaking them to the judges. They won't respond, but give the lines time to breathe, as if they might anyway," Ms. Brophy had said. "And most importantly, be honest and brave. Be *you*, Brie."

"Gabrielle Hutchens?" called a woman with a clipboard.

Brie and her mom had been waiting for only about twenty minutes. Brie had thought they would have longer.

The two of them stood and followed the woman with the clipboard through a doorway that led to the auditorium. Brie had left her phone in the car—they'd been told not to bring them in—and she wished that she could text Parker or Wallace or . . . or Kennedy. Just to feel like something else existed outside this room.

"You're Gabrielle's mom?" the woman asked, and Brie's mom nodded. "You can sit here, in the back, if you want to watch. We just ask that you remain silent throughout the audition."

"Oh, I can wait outside if—"

"No," Brie interrupted, her heart in her throat. "Just . . . stay here, okay?"

Her mom slowly nodded and took a seat.

The woman with the clipboard turned to Brie. "Okay. I'm going to lead you to the stage. The panel of judges is in the front row. Say your name and what you're going to perform, and then just begin when you're ready."

She showed Brie where the stairs to the stage were, and as Brie walked up each step, she looked around the auditorium in awe. It was nothing like the stage at OLPH. It wasn't like being with her classmates, dressed as Grumpy. Parker wasn't onstage with her. Her dad hadn't painted any sets. And the lines she was going to say—unlike the silly ones in *Snow White*—were personal and deep. They were rehearsed—she would be acting—but they were real. They were too real.

These lines had started everything.

She walked to center stage, and a spotlight shone brightly in her eyes, making her hot and making it impossible to see her mom or the judges right in front of her. The theater was large and quiet, and Brie felt completely alone. "My name is Gabrielle Hutchens. Um, you can call me Brie." Her fingers were fidgeting at her sides, and she tried her hardest to keep them still. "I'm doing a scene from, uh, *All My Children*. The soap opera. Between Bianca and her mom." She paused and then added, "I'm playing Bianca."

Brie stood there, waiting awkwardly, before she remembered that the lady with the clipboard had told her to just
begin whenever she was ready. It felt weird, and she knew
she must look pink and sweaty, and her pulse was beating
loudly in her ears. But she'd done this before. Not just this
monologue, but this conversation. She'd had it with Parker,
with her dad, with Travis. With Ms. Brophy and Ms. Santos.
With Kennedy.

She would have it again and again, she was learning.
And she needed her mom to finally hear it. She needed her
mom to *see* her.

Nothing will change if you stop trying, Brie thought and
took a deep breath.

"This isn't me, Mom," Brie began as rehearsed. "It
never was."

Ms. Brophy had told her to look straight out at the back
of the auditorium, over the judges' heads. That's where Brie's
mom was.

"I have to tell you something. Look at me. Look at me!
I want you to see who I am, Mother. Can you see who I am?
Can you?" Brie's voice cracked, and she let it. She let her nose
burn and her eyes fill with tears. "I'm trying to show you."

She paused, closed her eyes, and breathed through her
nose. The judges would not respond. Her mom would not
respond. Brie wished they would. She wished they would
just . . . say something. She wished her mom would *say*

something. "Have you always loved me, Mom?" she continued. The silence—though expected because her mom had been instructed to keep quiet—took Brie's breath away, anyway. "Do you love me now?"

The sudden noise of the auditorium doors at the back of the room swinging open and creaking closed made Brie flinch. The light was still in her eyes; she couldn't see anything. "Do you?" she repeated.

Tears dripped down her cheeks.

She could only whisper those last words: "I'm gay."

$$\text{\Large\ast}$$

Brie knew her mom was no longer at the back of the auditorium, but as she left the room, wiping furiously at her cheeks, she was surprised that her mom wasn't in the hallway, either. Brie thought she'd have to borrow someone's phone to call her dad to pick her up, but when she went outside, her mom was waiting in the car.

Brie walked to the passenger side and climbed in. She shut the door, and her mom asked, "All done, then?"

Brie nodded, strapping her seat belt on.

Her mom drove. Brie sat back and watched the houses and trees and cars and telephone wires go by. She wondered if this was it. If, again, everything that should be said would go unsaid. If she could shout all the things she needed to say from center stage, and her mom would still ignore what she said.

But before they made it even halfway home, her mom pulled the car over to the side of the road. She turned off the ignition, and Brie said nothing, just watched her mom, confused.

And then her mom buried her face in her hands and started to cry.

Brie inhaled sharply. She couldn't remember the last time she'd seen her mom cry. Had she *ever* seen her mom cry? Her mom was always the pillar of strength in their house, the boss, the "bad guy," the one who held them all together even when her dad was sad and tired and mopey. She didn't think anything could make her mom crumble, but she was wrong, because apparently *she* could.

"Mom?" Brie said, her own voice cracked and wobbly.

"What the hell, Brie?" her mom said, face still buried, voice strained.

Fresh tears spilled from Brie's eyes. "I just . . ." She didn't know what to say.

Her mom sniffed heavily and picked her head up, pulling down the sun visor to look at her face in the mirror. "God, I'm a mess."

"I'm sorry," Brie said, though she didn't know what for. She'd just felt the impulse to say it, couldn't have held it in even if she'd wanted to.

"Okay," her mom said, sitting back and pushing the visor up. "Okay. Let's talk about this."

"Really?"

"I don't know what you want me to say," her mom said. "I don't know how to do this. I don't know how to connect with you. You're so young. You're too young. Are you sure?"

There was a desperate note in her mom's voice that Brie hated. "I think so."

"You think so? You don't even know?"

"No, I know," Brie said. "I just . . . don't know everything? It's confusing, Mom. You know it's confusing. You know why I was on the computer looking at all that stuff. You made it worse. I wasn't ready. You made it happen because you looked at my laptop, and then you wouldn't even talk to me about it. That sucked, Mom."

"You were acting so weird. I was worried," her mom said. "I had no idea. And I don't . . . God, Brie, I don't want this for you. No mom wants their child to have to go through life with more difficulty than they have to. I don't want you to get hurt."

Brie frowned. "*This* hurts. *This* is what hurts me."

Her mom buried her face again.

Brie pulled down her own visor. The sun was bright in front of them, and it was just a reminder to Brie how weird it was to finally be having this conversation, even more so to be having it on the side of the road, in the middle of the day, in public. She slouched in her seat. "I know you don't like me," she said. "But I'm still hoping that you can be okay with this."

Her mom turned to stare at Brie, her mouth open. "What do you mean I don't . . . Brie, I love you."

Brie shrugged. "Yeah, I know. But I mean, you don't . . . *like* me. It's different. I'm different. And not just because of . . . this. I've never really been what you wanted me to."

Her mom kept staring at her. "Is that why you lied about . . ." She suddenly reached forward, placing her palm against Brie's cheek as she leaned in close and met Brie's eyes with her own. "You listen to me, Gabrielle. I love you. I *like* you. I don't always get you, but God, Brie, I wouldn't trade you in for anything."

It sounded nice. It sounded like everything her mom should be saying. But still . . . Brie wasn't sure. "You still haven't said it's okay."

"What?"

"I like Kennedy Bishop, Mom. *Like* her, like her. I don't think she likes me anymore, because I was sort of mean, but she did, for a bit. And Parker knew. And, well, Dad and Trevor knew. But I really . . . need you to know, too."

"God, Brie. But aren't you . . . a little young for that?"

"You didn't think I was too young for boys," Brie pointed out.

"Right. You're right," her mom said. "I just think I need some time with this."

Brie shook her head. "No. You've had so much time, Mom. It's either okay or it's not!"

"Please, Brie. I just . . ." She sighed. "I'm trying, okay? Just . . . just let me keep trying."

It had been months since her mom had looked at Brie's computer and seen into her head and learned all the things Brie was struggling with. She hadn't tried then, had she? Or when Brie had messed up the May Crowning and shouted things at her mom, had she tried then? How was Brie supposed to know if she ever really would? How could Brie be sure they wouldn't get back to the house and continue not talking about it, that they wouldn't go back to pushing it aside?

"No," Brie said. "Not until you say it. Not until you promise me it'll be okay."

Cars drove past. Birds sang. Life went on around them.

But everything stopped for Brie as she held her mom's gaze, waiting.

And then finally—*finally*—her mom reached out.

She pulled Brie into a hug over the center console of the car. It was uncomfortable and awkward, but Brie wouldn't have moved for the world. "Okay," her mom said. "Okay. It'll all be okay."

How were auditions?

Brie saw the text after she and her mom got home. She didn't reply. She wanted to—she didn't want Kennedy to think she was ignoring her again—but God, where to start?

Sitting in church the next day with her family was . . . weird. She wanted to be able to respond when she was supposed to respond, and sing along to the church songs, but she felt funny sitting there. Her throat was tight and scratchy, and nothing came out.

Her mom was quieter than usual, too. She didn't seem to be responding to much, either, and her silence made her seem more distracted than deep in prayer.

Brie sat between her mom and dad, Trevor in the seat next to the aisle, and she felt smaller than usual between them. Last night her mom had kissed her good night, and her dad had asked at least four times if she was okay, but the air was just harder to breathe when she was near them.

The priest stood, and the parishioners followed. Brie's eyes found the statue of Mary from the May Crowning, still wearing her flower crown. The one Kennedy had placed on her head. *Hail Mary, full of grace.*

Brie bet Kennedy had looked beautiful up on the altar that day.

Brie's dad reached over to take Brie's hand, and Brie jumped, startled by the contact. She looked up at him, and he offered her a smile as he squeezed her hand. She leaned her body to rest against his.

Holy Mary, Mother of God. Brie wondered if Mary had ever been . . . disappointed in Jesus, and if he really had grown up the way she'd expected him to. She wondered what would have happened if he hadn't—if all the things the angels had promised Mary had turned out *not* to be true. Would she have loved him anyway?

Had they ever argued? Had she ever made him mad? Had he felt like she really saw him, the real him?

Brie remembered being in second grade and practicing for her First Communion, sitting in the chapel, listening to Sister Patricia tell a story about when Jesus was as little as they were. His parents, Mary and Joseph, took him to a festival. Afterward, he went missing.

Brie didn't know if Mary had ever been disappointed or angry, but Sister Patricia told them how Mary had been afraid. Jesus had scared her when they couldn't find him that day.

They finally found him in the temple. When they told him that he'd frightened them, that they had been anxiously looking, he told them he was exactly where he was supposed to be.

For her entire life—or at least since kindergarten—Brie had woken up, put on her pleated skirt, buttoned up her dress shirt, and gone to Catholic school, where every classroom had its own cross. They went to mass every Friday. They took religion tests, got graded on their knowledge of faith. Her mom prayed before meals when the family was all together. They celebrated Christmas and Easter and got black marks on their foreheads for Ash Wednesday. They didn't eat meat on Fridays during Lent.

Brie looked over at her mom, who was so quiet, so still. Was her mom looking up at that altar—at that cross and at Mary—thinking all the same things? Or was she thinking about Brie and how much harder Brie's life might be now? Was she thinking about how unaccepting this place, where she'd always sought solace, could be?

Brie's phone was buried deep in her pocket, Kennedy's text still unanswered. *How were auditions?*

Brie looked again at her mother.

She wished she was closer to knowing the answers.

June

Two Saturdays until
the Dinner Dance

23.

ALL MY CHILDREN, December 2000:
Bianca tries to come out to her mom. Her mom
does not listen . . . but eventually she does.
Eventually, both of them turn out okay.

"Okay, but if you do get in, are you going to go?" Parker asked after Brie had explained the whole ordeal. "And if you don't, are you definitely *not* going to Red Bank Catholic?"

Brie laughed. "You'll still be my best friend, no matter where I go."

"Promise?" Parker asked, holding out her pinkie.

Brie put her sandwich down so she could hook her finger with Parker's. "Promise."

"I hope you and your mom are okay," Parker said, passing her Cheetos to Brie. Parker hated getting orange-dust fingers. Brie didn't mind. "I always just figured if your parents weren't bigots or whatever, like if they didn't disown you or throw you out, things were okay. I didn't realize it'd be so hard for you."

Brie sighed. "I'm really glad my mom and dad love me and for the most part accept me. Really, I am. I'm lucky—I know that."

"*But* . . ." Parker prompted.

"But everything still hurt. *Hurts.* I don't know. I know people have it worse, but I wish it wasn't so sucky. It's still not okay."

"I'm really sorry, Brie," Parker said.

The cafeteria was loud as always, and Parker and Brie sat at the tail end of one of the eighth-grade girls' lunch tables, the one that had the best view of the boys. Parker was currently staring at them.

Brie turned to look at them, too, just as Jack Thomas noticed Parker and lifted his hand in a small wave. Parker turned pink, waved back, and then used that hand to tuck her hair behind her ear in a not-very-casual way. Brie laughed.

Parker sighed. "I'm going to have to just . . . do it."

"Do what?" Brie asked.

"Ask someone to the dinner dance."

"Oh!" Brie said, turning back to the table where Jack, Javi, and Wallace sat. "Who are you going to ask?"

"Good question."

Brie laughed again.

"How about you?" Parker asked, then leaned in and lowered her voice to a whisper. "Anything happen lately between you and Kennedy?"

Brie quickly shook her head. "Wallace said he'd go with me as friends. I'm just going to do that. Kennedy and I are barely talking, and besides, I don't really want to give my mom or Sister Patricia a stroke by taking another girl as my date."

"But you *are* talking again?" Parker asked. "You and Kennedy, I mean."

Brie cringed. "I mean, a few texts. Does that even count? I think I screwed it all up. She'll probably go to RBC with you next year, anyway."

"Oh come on," Parker said. "You just came out to your mom, for real, in the middle of an audition! You gave a monologue in front of Ms. Brophy and Ms. Santos about being a slut!"

"The Slut of Springfield," Brie corrected. "And I think the character was being sarcastic when she said that."

"My point is, since when do you shrink away from a challenge? You watch soap operas, Brie, and you love every second of them. You want to be a soap star. You *love* being dramatic."

"Yeah, but . . . what's your point?"

"A few texts? Oh, Brie." Parker laughed and threw a Cheeto at Brie's face. "You can do much, much better than that."

Come three o'clock that afternoon, Brie's mom was in the living room, watching *General Hospital* like normal. Or, well, like what used to be their normal. Brie lingered in the kitchen, pretending to be looking for a snack. She grabbed a Pop-Tart and moved to linger in the doorway instead.

She didn't wait for a commercial. "Mom?"

"Yeah?"

"The eighth-grade-graduation dinner dance is coming up," Brie said. "I need a new dress. I mean, I guess technically no one really saw me much in my May Crowning dress but . . . I was kinda hoping we could go shopping for a new one anyway." She paused before adding, "If it's too much money, that's okay."

"No, no," her mom said, reaching for the remote to mute the TV. "We can do that. This weekend? I have Sunday off."

Brie nodded. "Yeah, okay."

Usually, this was the moment when her mom would ask her about boys and dancing with boys and going to dances with boys. Instead, she smiled and turned the volume back up on the TV. Brie wasn't sure whether that was better or worse.

When they did go shopping, Brie regretted asking to go at all as she tried on her fifth dress, already knowing she was going to hate it. "It's pink."

"Salmon. And nearly half the dresses in this store are. It's the color of the year, Brie—I didn't choose it," her mom said. "What about the purple one?"

Brie opened the fitting room door to shoot her mom a look. "I looked like an eggplant."

"You're impossible."

"These dresses are impossible!"

"Just try on the rest, please."

Brie groaned and grabbed another dress from the pile before closing the fitting room door. Her mom stood—a little too closely, in Brie's opinion—outside of it. Brie could see her shoes through the opening at the bottom of the door. She took off the salmon-colored dress to put on a light-green one. She shimmied it over her hips and struggled to pull up the zipper. "Hey, Mom? Can I ask you a question?"

"If it's about my taste in dresses, no."

Brie rolled her eyes. "Did you and Dad ever get into a fight that you knew was your fault, like when you knew you hurt his feelings, and you said sorry, but things still didn't really feel okay?"

She heard her mom say "Hmm" from the other side of the door. "I mean, we've gotten into fights where I was in the wrong, sure. I guess when your dad lost his job, I had a hard time figuring out how to say the right thing. I think I made things worse a lot of the time, trying to just . . . figure out the practicalities instead of focusing on how he was doing."

"Did you *eventually* focus on how he was doing?"

"When I realized how sad and tired he was all the time? Of course."

"Did it just . . . get better, then?"

"Do you need help getting that dress on?" her mom asked. Brie opened the door and turned around so her mom could help with the zipper. "It's a work in progress. Your dad is trying really hard to figure out what comes next for him. I still have to focus on the practicalities. You and Trevor both need to do your part. Sometimes relationships take work and time. You can't always understand exactly how the other person is feeling. But if you mess up, you listen. You figure out why you messed up in the first place. You promise to do better."

Her mom smoothed out the side of the dress and took a step back so they both could look at it in the mirror. Brie did not hate it. "Am I a work in progress?"

Her mom laughed. "We all are, Brie."

"I messed up with someone I like. And I've been trying really hard to fix it."

"I know the feeling." Her mom's voice was soft. "I think this dress looks beautiful."

Brie nodded. "I think so, too."

"Then take it off so I can get it for you."

They still weren't *really* talking about it. But it was the most Brie had confided in her mom about Kennedy. It felt like progress—even if she didn't know what to do with the advice—and *that* made every salmon-colored dress worth it.

✳

Ms. Brophy was out of breath after running down the hallway to catch up with Brie and her dad as they were getting ready to leave school the next day. "I'm so glad I caught you!" she said.

Her dad looked appropriately startled. Brie did not. It was the last month of the school year, so Brie was used to Ms. Brophy by now. "Hi, Diane, what's going on?" Brie's dad asked.

Ms. Brophy placed both hands on Brie's shoulders and squeezed. "I have great news!"

"Oh. Cool," Brie said, sending a sideways glance her dad's way. He looked as if he was close to laughing.

"I heard from a colleague at MCPA that you had one of the more impressive auditions of the day!" Ms. Brophy said.

Brie's jaw dropped. "I had *what* now?"

"Now, I can't say anything officially, but *unofficially*, I think you should keep your eyes out for a certain email

251

soon. You should be really proud of yourself. I know you worked very hard on your audition." Ms. Brophy smiled up at Brie's dad and then winked at Brie. "And then some." She gave Brie's shoulder one last squeeze and then continued down the hallway to the main office.

"Wow," her dad said. "That's great, kid. Guess we're going to have to cross that bridge and have that conversation now, huh?"

If Brie had learned anything this year, it was not to count her chickens before they hatched (or lie about them to begin with). Sister Patricia might not agree, but sometimes seeing really *was* necessary for believing. She would wait until she saw that email herself before she got too excited.

(Well, okay. She was already pretty excited. She was human, after all.)

But when she looked at her dad, she knew there was something she needed to say. "It's okay if I can't go, Dad. I won't be mad, I won't blame you, if we can't afford it."

He bent down to look into her eyes. His were wrinkled and bright. His eyelashes were gray. "Let's just see what we can do."

Ms. Brophy says I unofficially got in. Brie finally responded to Kennedy's text. *I'm trying not to get my hopes up too high. Easier said than done.*

There was no response, and Brie figured she deserved that. She kept texting anyway. Giving up wouldn't change anything. *Sorry I didn't respond. The auditions weren't good. I mean, they clearly were good. But I sort of came out to my mom and the judges during it, and my mom didn't exactly take that well.*

This time, the response was almost instantaneous. *You did what?? Is everything ok? What happened!!*

Kennedy's concern made Brie feel tingly, but she figured if anyone could understand the feelings that sometimes gripped Brie's throat, it was her. *Things were weird. But they've been weird for a while and I think they're finally getting better.*

She paused and then added, *I hope so anyway.*

Nothing else was forthcoming, and Brie figured that was it. But then her phone buzzed again. *I don't think I could ever tell my mom*, Kennedy's text read.

It made Brie want to cry. Not just because Kennedy was clearly worried about it, but because Brie had never stopped to think about Kennedy's specific struggles. That Kennedy was realizing the same things about herself, that Kennedy had a family who might not be okay with it, and that she might not know what to do. Kennedy understood the confusion and the hurt and the fear and the nerves, and Brie had never asked her about it. *I'm sorry*, Brie wrote. *But maybe you can tell her someday.*

Maybe, Kennedy responded. *But I'm not ready to find out.*

Brie never felt ready, no matter how many times she had to say the words. She hoped that Kennedy would figure out how to do it on her own time. She hoped that when she did it, it would be because she *was* ready. Not because she felt pressured to.

In the meantime, Brie wanted to be there to find out. *I like you*, Brie texted. *I didn't know how to say it but now I do. I know we can't go to the dinner dance together and I know you might not even want to because I screwed up so much. But I wanted you to know that anyway. Are you going to the dance?*

Brie held her breath as she waited for a response. Or, at least, she held her breath until she needed oxygen. Kennedy took a long time.

I'm going, her text read.

Brie did a little happy dance under her comforter. *Good. Let's talk then*, Brie wrote and then closed out the conversation to text Parker.

It was a rare night when everyone was home to eat dinner together. Brie was getting used to being in charge of meals, so she was almost annoyed that her mom had decided to make chili. Brie hated beans. Her mom used so many.

"We have some things we need to talk about," Brie's mom began after they said grace.

Trevor chewed a mouthful of chili—he loved beans—as he asked, "What about now?"

Their parents exchanged glances, and Brie watched as her mom raised her eyebrows at her dad. He was clearly supposed to be the one speaking. "Well," her mom continued when he didn't. "OLPH asked your dad to stay on as maintenance. With Brie graduating, he'll get a full salary from them."

Brie looked at her dad. "Do you like working there?"

He smiled at her. "I do. And Diane Brophy already asked if I'd help with sets again next year, and I'd really like to. The only thing I'll be missing is you."

"Trevor, your father and I want to start talking about college this summer. We think that maybe you should consider two years at the community college," their mom said.

Trevor pulled a face. "Do we need to talk about this now?"

"No," their dad said. "But this summer we will. Just know that we'll help you figure out financial aid and student loans, but we want you to consider the cheaper options, too. Especially since you're not sure what you want to do yet."

"I'll figure it out," Trevor said.

"We know you will," their mom said. "We just want you to know there's nothing wrong with figuring that out in community college."

"In the meantime, we've also decided you're going to park in the street. You'll be responsible for paying attention to the snow and street-cleaning rules, but your days of messing up my lawn are over," her dad said.

Trevor sighed but didn't argue.

"Brie," her mom started.

Brie sighed. "Public high school, I know, I know."

Her parents exchanged glances again. "We're going to wait for the official email," her mom said. "And we'll see what they expect us to pay, and we'll talk to the arts school about scholarships and funding. We'll take it a step at a time."

"But . . ." Brie prompted.

"*But*," her dad repeated. "We really want to try."

Brie couldn't believe it. All the hard work and confusion, and the mess of the last few months . . .

But she'd learned a thing or two in those months, too. "Just . . . don't try too hard, okay, Dad? I know you do a lot. I know you and Mom get tired a lot. I'll be okay if we can't."

He reached across the table for her hand. "But if we can?" he asked.

Brie smiled. She couldn't help it. "Then move over, Susan Lucci! I'm going to be an actress."

Brie was in the light-green dress, looking at herself in the mirror. She was meeting Wallace and Parker at school. They'd decided to all go to the dance together.

There was a knock on her bedroom door. Brie turned to find her mom standing at the threshold. "You look beautiful, Gabrielle."

Brie looked back at her reflection in the mirror. "Do you think I look different?"

"Different how?" her mom asked.

"I don't know," Brie said. "I just . . . feel really different. But I also feel exactly the same."

"In the dress?"

"In general." Brie pursed her lips. "I'm going to kiss a girl tonight."

"Oh Jesus," her mom said, walking over to Brie's bed. "Let me sit down. Please do not get thrown out of the dance tonight. And please make sure this other . . . girl . . . wants to be kissed before you do anything."

Brie scoffed. "Of course, I'm not an idiot."

Her mom stood up from the bed and walked over to where Brie was standing. She grew quiet, hesitating, before she reached into her pocket.

Brie didn't know how she felt when her mom pulled her hand out and her Mary pendant was bright and silver and shining in her palm. "I know that you're still, well, figuring things out. And maybe these things aren't as important to you, and really, that's okay," her mom said, fidgeting with the metal in her fingers. "But it's important to me. And—you don't have to wear it, ever, if you don't want to—but I just really want you to have it."

Brie held out her hand, and her mom dropped the pendant into it. Brie ran her fingers over the surface. She didn't know if she would ever wear it again. Right then, it really didn't matter. It felt, oddly, like the olive branch she had been waiting for.

Brie looked back at the mirror. She asked again, "Do you think I look different, Mom?"

Her mom reached for Brie's hair, swooping it back behind her shoulders as she ran her fingers through the strands. "You look like Brie," she said, shrugging. "And a little like your dad."

"As long as I don't have his nose," Brie said.

Her mom didn't laugh like Brie thought she might. Instead, she leaned down to kiss the top of Brie's head before focusing her attention on their reflections. Brie's eyes met her mom's in the mirror. "Just . . . be careful, okay?" her mom said. "All I want is for you to just be careful."

24.

REAL LIFE, this year: Brie Hutchens (me) has her first crush on a girl, and comes out to her mom, and her dad, and her brother, and her best friend, and and and . . . Everything sucks.

. . . But then Brie gets brave. Then her mom starts to see her. Then everything gets better.

The auditorium that was a gym, a theater, and a church was transformed that night into a ballroom for the eighth-grade dinner dance.

Brie stood at the entrance, looking in at the fairy lights twinkling along the walls and ceiling, at the tables covered in gold tablecloths, at the bright, colorful lights by the DJ on the dance floor. The classmates she was used to seeing in their plaid uniform skirts or blue slacks and polo shirts were dressed up in shimmering dresses or ironed suits, their hair

259

done. The boys looked clean. Everything looked fancier than a room inside their school building should be.

Parker stood next to her, in a pale-pink dress that matched the color of her cheeks. "Our last OLPH school dance," she said.

Wallace wobbled up the stairs on his crutches to join them, his tie untied around his neck. "Ready to knock 'em dead?" he said.

Once inside, Brie immediately started scanning the room for Kennedy, and Parker looked around for either Jack or Javi—she'd decided whomever she saw first would be the one she would ask to dance. Wallace went right to the buffet.

"There's Jack!" Parker said, pointing across the dance floor.

Brie shoved her with her shoulder. "Go on, then. It's time to finally act! Last school dance, you said it yourself!"

Parker took a deep breath. "Okay, okay. But you better keep looking for Kennedy!"

She left, and Brie was alone. The music was loud, her classmates were louder, and for a large auditorium, it was getting pretty stuffy. Brie felt sweat on the back of her neck.

There was a tap on her shoulder that made her jump. Ms. Santos laughed as they came face-to-face. "Whoa, didn't mean to scare you."

Ms. Santos was wearing a deep-blue dress. It had pockets, and one of her hands was tucked deep inside one. Brie was flustered by being startled and by how good Ms. Santos looked standing there. She could barely get her words out. Some things would never change.

"Right. Hi. Yeah."

Ms. Santos laughed again. "I wanted to make sure I got a chance to snag you before you got caught up dancing. I started figuring out grades for the last marking period, and, well, I purposely sat down to do yours first."

"Uh-oh," Brie said. "Do I even want to know?"

"Half a year of excellent work doesn't totally make up for the other half of slacking off, but you just barely pulled a solid B. Which is better than the C you were destined for at the start of the school year," Ms. Santos said.

"That's awesome!" Brie said. "My mom'll be . . ."

That was when she noticed Kennedy standing on the other side of the room, in a purple dress that matched the purple knit cap—which Brie loved—that she'd worn all winter. Kennedy's fingers were fidgeting and folding into one another, and she shifted her weight from one foot to the other and back again as she looked around the room.

"Ms. Santos, thanks—for everything," Brie said. "But I have one more favor to ask."

Ms. Santos leaned conspiratorially toward her. "What do you need?"

"I need you to distract Sister Patricia. For at least an entire song."

"You're not going to, like, pull a fire alarm or something, are you?" Ms. Santos asked.

Brie shook her head. "Nothing bad. Promise. There's just

261

something I gotta fix, because I messed things up, but a certain teacher of mine once told me not to give up."

Ms. Santos practically rolled her eyes, though she kept smiling. "Using my words against me. All right, all right. Just for you, just this once."

Brie could have hugged Ms. Santos right then and there—if she hadn't thought it would actually make her explode inside.

With Ms. Santos off to keep Sister Patricia occupied (the last thing Brie needed was Sister Patricia walking around the dance floor, telling everyone to "leave room for the Holy Spirit"), Brie searched again for Kennedy. When Kennedy's eyes met Brie's, Brie lifted her hand in a small wave. Kennedy smiled but didn't move.

"You gonna go get the girl or what?" Wallace said, suddenly creeping up beside her. "You've been moping over her for months. Just do it already."

He was annoying, but he was right. Brie needed to stop waiting, stop worrying. "Just watch me," she told Wallace, and she crossed the floor to Kennedy.

"Hi," she said when she was close enough.

"Hi," Kennedy said.

Brie refused to wait for the silence to settle awkwardly between them, as it had for much too long already. "I have something to tell you."

Kennedy's eyebrows pinched together. "Oh?"

"I like you," Brie said. "I mean, *really* like you. I have for a while, and I messed it all up. You drive me crazy that you're so good at everything, but I know that just because you're good at stuff doesn't mean you've got it easy. If anything, you're just as confused and messed up as me, because I think you like me, too, or at least I hope you still do, because this will be really awkward and terrible if you don't." Brie took a deep breath, checked to make sure Ms. Santos was following through, and hold out her hand. "So let's hope for my mom's sake we don't get in trouble, but will you please dance with me?"

"*Here?*" Kennedy asked. "Now?"

Brie nodded. "Here. Now."

Kennedy hesitated, and Brie let her. She knew all too well that Kennedy Bishop was worth waiting for. And then Kennedy nodded and took Brie's hand.

The week before, on *General Hospital*, one of the teenage characters danced with the boy of her dreams at her prom. They looked so perfect together. Everyone else turned to watch them as they spun in circles around the dance floor. They were made king and queen.

Another student set the banquet hall on fire later, but that wasn't the point. It was a soap opera, after all.

Brie thought about that moment, that dance, as she and Kennedy made their way to the floor. They had an awkward moment where neither one knew exactly where she should put her hands. Kennedy settled hers on Brie's shoulders, so

Brie put hers on Kennedy's waist. She was pretty sure they were shaking.

Everyone didn't stop and look at them. The few who did were more confused than anything. Parker gave a thumbs-up from behind Jack's back as she danced with him, and Wallace smiled at her from the buffet.

"My mom was worried I was going to get us thrown out of the dance," Brie said.

"My mom doesn't know how I feel about you," Kennedy replied.

Brie felt those familiar pins and needles once again. "How do you feel about me?"

Kennedy's smile was shy, her eyes looked down at her toes, and that strand of hair was loose, just waiting for Brie to fix it. So she did. She reached out and tucked it behind Kennedy's ear.

"It's true," Kennedy said. "I really like you, too."

Brie didn't know where she would end up next year. She didn't know if her mom would ever be okay with her bringing Kennedy or someone else over to the house for dinner, or to her room. She figured her door would always have to stay open.

Right now, though, none of that mattered. Not with the way Kennedy was looking at her. Not with the way her mom had hugged her before she'd left.

Tonight, all that mattered was that Brie and Kennedy had shared that kiss.

Acknowledgments

Everyone warns about how difficult writing the second book can be, but I've been blessed with a team of people who have made this as easy and enjoyable as possible.

I know that everyone says they have the best agent, but unless they also have Jim McCarthy, they are wrong. Jim, you've been the best champion of my work from the start, and I couldn't ask for a better person to share this journey with.

I may have wanted to scream every time my editor, Krestyna Lypen, asked me to add a new chapter and sent me farther down the soap opera rabbit hole, but she was right every time, even if I wanted her to be wrong so I could be lazy. Krestyna's editorial eye pushed me to pull out the things in the manuscript I had skirted around, and made me go deeper and really tell the story I was telling. I'm more than thankful for that, even if it did give me minor Catholic-school PTSD.

Elise Howard, you promised me from the start that Algonquin would take good care of me and my work, and this has been proven over and over again to be 100 percent true. Megan Harley, Carla Bruce-Eddings, Ashley Mason, Sarah Alpert, Carla Weise, Laura Williams, Kristen Bianco, Kelly Doyle, and my entire AYR team: thank you for keeping it real, keeping my anxiety low, and making everything about this process a total blast. Caitlin Rubinstein: you are the Zeke to my Jimmy Jr., and I am forever grateful to be able to call you my friend.

Mom and Dad, thank you for the cupcakes (among *everything* else)! Do I get more for this book?

Liz Welch, you are, as always, my Theo and my wuffenloaf.